BIBI AND THE
BOX OF FAIRY TALES

This is a Zephyr book, first published in the UK in 2023
by Head of Zeus Ltd, part of Bloomsbury Publishing Plc

9 7 5 3 1 2 4 6 8

A catalogue record for this book is available from the British Library.

ISBN (HB): 9781803289731
ISBN (E): 9781803289717

Designed by Jessie Price

Printed and Bound in Slovenia by DZS Grafik d.o.o.

Head of Zeus Ltd
First Floor East
5–8 Hardwick Street
London EC1R 4RG
WWW.HEADOFZEUS.COM

BIBI AND THE BOX
OF FAIRY TALES

VIVIAN FRENCH ILLUSTRATED BY AMY GRIMES

ZEPHYR
an imprint of Head of Zeus

For Nancy and Guillem,
with very much love. xxx
— VF

For Harry.
— AG

CONTENTS

MEETiNG MiSs MYRTLE

Bibi stared at her new home.

When her mum said they were moving to a house in the woods, she had imagined a thatched cottage with roses nodding a welcome beside the door. Instead, the chimney was crooked, the roof sagged, and the walls were draped in ivy. A single dandelion offered the only splash of colour.

But then the sun came out from behind the clouds and the windows twinkled cheerfully. Bibi looked at the cottage again. There was a twisted tower at one end; could that be her room? It might be fun to sleep up high, like a bird in its nest.

'Have you got the key, Mum?' she asked.

Her mother pulled a large key from her bag. 'I don't think anybody's lived here for a long time,' she said. 'Maybe it's been waiting for us?'

As the key turned in the lock, Bibi whispered, 'Please let it be all right, please!'

And the door swung open.

·ʾ✳·ʾ·

The hall was narrow, and it felt... *odd*, Bibi thought. *It's... it's as if the house is excited...* In the first room she found armchairs so worn it was impossible to tell their colour, and a lace of spiders' webs at the window.

'Mum! Come and sit down!' she called.

As her mother sank into a chair, a cloud of dust made Bibi sneeze.

'I'll find the kitchen and make a cup of tea.'

'Thank you, pet,' her mum said. 'What would I do without you?'

As she hurried from the room, Bibi thought *Maybe I'll check upstairs first? It won't take long...*

And so Bibi began to explore. There were two bedrooms with a bathroom in

between; the ivy covering the windows turned the sunlight dim and green. *And now for the tower room...* The stair to the tower twisted round and round until Bibi felt dizzy. *It seems an awfully long way*, she thought... but still the stairs went on. At last, just as she was beginning to think she would climb for ever, Bibi found herself in front of a door. Turning the handle she walked in – and gasped.

·٠✳٠·

Sitting in an upright chair was the strangest old woman Bibi had ever seen. She was so grey she was almost invisible, but when she spoke her voice was as sharp as a needle.

'You're here at last! Took your time, didn't you?'

Bibi blinked. 'Who... who are you?'

'Myrtle Hartleberry. Miss Myrtle to you. I'm your fairy godmother.'

'You can't be.' Bibi folded her arms. 'I don't believe in fairies. And I hate fairy stories. All those stupid princesses and pumpkins and ugly beasts that are princes in disguise.'

Miss Myrtle sniffed. 'How very foolish. Why do you think fairy stories have lasted so long? You can learn a lot from them... if you want to, of course.'

'Well, I don't want to,' Bibi snapped. The old woman's outline was now so faint Bibi wondered if she was a ghost. *But ghosts don't talk like that, she told herself. Like... like a cross schoolteacher.*

'What are you doing here?' she asked.

'I'm your fairy godmother. And fairy godmothers grant wishes.'

'Only babies believe in that kind of thing,' Bibi said. 'I've tried wishing for things over and over, and nothing ever happens.

'And what, exactly, were you wishing for?' Miss Myrtle asked.

Bibi wanted to say, *mind your own business*, but there was something about the fierce old lady that made her pause.

'I want us to stay in one place. I'm sick of having to move around all the time ...' To her annoyance, Bibi found that she wanted to cry. Swallowing the feeling down, she said, 'So there.'

'I see.' Miss Myrtle nodded. 'Well, you'd better get busy.' She pointed to the darkest corner. 'If you can

open that box, you'll have a wish that comes true. It won't be easy, mind.' Her voice softened. 'But I suspect you're not afraid of hard work?'

Bibi didn't answer. She was looking at the box, surprised she hadn't noticed it before. It was *glowing* and painted a glorious scarlet, with swirls of gold and silver flowers... But Miss Myrtle was right: opening it *wasn't* going to be easy. Wrapped round the box were seven chains, each with a different padlock.

'What's inside?' Bibi asked. Miss Myrtle cackled with laughter.

'That's for you to find out! If you earn seven keys I promise – and a fairy godmother's promise is one to trust – you shall have a wish. What's more, the box will be yours to keep.'

'Huh.' Bibi tried to sound disbelieving. She didn't care about the wish; she knew that was impossible – but the box was the most beautiful thing she had ever seen. 'If I said yes – and I most probably won't – what kind of thing would I have to do?'

'Enter the world of fairy stories,' said Miss Myrtle, folding her hands in her lap.

Bibi made a face. 'All that stuff about going on quests?'

The fairy godmother raised her eyebrows. 'If you succeed in a quest, my dear, you'll earn a key. Earn seven keys... and you'll open the box.'

Bibi stared.

Miss Myrtle took off her spectacles and tucked them into a pocket. 'It's your decision. If you return, you'll find your way to the first story. One last thing... look out for Sylvestro. He'll keep you company...' and with that Miss Myrtle Hartleberry disappeared. All that was left was her chair, and as Bibi looked round, she saw the box had also vanished. In its place was... she rubbed her eyes. Had she seen the skulking shadow of a cat?

'It's all a dream,' she told herself. 'It has to be.' But, as she went downstairs, she couldn't stop thinking, *could it – just possibly – be true?* A magical box... and a wish?

Bibi made her decision. She'd come back.

'And I bet the room's completely empty!' she said out loud... but even as she spoke, the tiniest of hopes was flickering in her mind.

DUST AND DRAGONS

n icy wind whipped the door open and Bibi stepped through.

'Hardly dressed for the weather, are we?'

Spinning round, she saw a large black cat sitting on a rock.

'Let's hope your adventures take you to sunnier places. I can't stand the cold myself.' He jumped down and took a step towards her. 'I'm Sylvestro. But first, let's get a couple of things clear. I do not wish to be stroked. And I do not wish to be called Puss.' He looked at Bibi to make sure she was listening. 'Now, I'm delighted to meet you.'

Bibi couldn't answer. Her head felt full of fluttering moths; one minute she had been walking up the stairs of a rickety old house, and here she was in a fairy-tale world where cats could talk.

She looked for the attic door – but it had vanished.

The cat was watching her. 'You won't find the door again. Not until you've completed your quest.' He twirled a whisker. 'So instead of gawping, I suggest you get on with it.'

Stung into action, Bibi looked about her.

·˙∗·ᵧ·

She was in a bleak valley where a fine dust covered everything. Flowers were trying to grow, but only the newest buds showed a glimpse of colour.

'It's as if the world's covered in soot,' she said, 'but there aren't any chimneys.'

Sylvestro jumped onto a rock and sneezed loudly. 'I wonder why Miss Myrtle sent us here?'

Bibi was wondering the same thing. The hills surrounding the valley towered against a heavy sky; there were no birds, no animals... no signs of life.

'Brrrrr!' she said, and she swung her arms to get warm. 'We need to find shelter.'

'Look!' Sylvestro waved a paw. 'Over there!'

Small figures dressed in black were sweeping away the soot and complaining loudly. They were tiny, but there was something strange about their shoulders... a shimmer and a gleam...

Bibi screwed up her eyes. 'Are they... could they be... they're surely not... *fairies*?' she asked.

'Quite possibly.' The cat didn't seem surprised.

'Maybe they can help us!'

Bibi began running towards them, but as soon as the fairies saw her, they hurried through an opening in the rocks. It was too narrow for Bibi to squeeze through. She could see a pile of brooms and a small, neat door, but no fairies.

'Please,' she called, 'can we talk?'

'What about?' The voice was not at all friendly.

Bibi hesitated. 'I need your help.'

'Why should we help you? We've got enough to do clearing this dust.' The second voice was as cross as the first. 'That scaredy giant hides away, and never lifts a finger.'

'That's right,' a third voice agreed. 'Scared of everything, he is! Even fairies!'

'We'll do a deal with you, human child.' It was the first voice again. 'You help us – then we'll talk about helping you.'

And the door slammed shut.

Bibi's eyes widened. Had she heard right? *A giant?* Her knees felt wobbly as she hurried back to Sylvestro crouching by his boulder.

'They said... they said there's a giant! Here in this valley!'

14

Sylvestro curled himself into a ball. 'Fairies, giants. Get used to it! We're in the world of fairy tales. So, what are you going to do?'

Bibi had no idea. She walked round the boulder to get out of the bite of the wind and give herself time to think. Leaning against its side, she shifted to make herself more comfortable. At once the boulder began to shake, and there was a strange rumbling sound. *It's like a giggle!* Bibi thought.

'Excuse me... but that tickles something dreadful!'

The voice was gruff, and Bibi jumped away. The boulder had grown a knobbly face with craggy eyebrows and a blob of a nose... but it was smiling, showing crooked teeth.

Bibi tried not to stare. 'Erm... hello,' she said.

The boulder heaved, and a bristly arm appeared. 'How do you do.' A large, weathered hand, several times the size of Bibi's, was held out. 'Glum.'

Bibi, wondering if her fingers would be crushed, shook Glum's thumb. 'How do you do. I'm Bibi. Erm... can I ask a question? Why is there dust everywhere?'

'It's the dragons.' Glum shivered, and a shower of stones rattled over Bibi. 'Whoops! Are you all right?'

But Bibi hardly noticed. '*Dragons*? In this valley?'

Glum lowered his voice to a rusty whisper. 'Yes, little lady. A family of dragons has moved in. They can't breathe fire, but they keep trying... the smoke goes up and up and turns into those black clouds. As for the soot... well. You can see for yourself!'

Bibi frowned. 'But surely a giant like you could chase the dragons away!'

'Me?' Glum began to tremble. 'Chase the dragons? No no no... dragons are ever so ever so scary!'

'Well... I think you should do *something*,' Bibi told him, 'otherwise you might be waiting for ever. Why don't—'

A thunder of wings beat in the sky. Glum, with a terrified yell, turned into a boulder; Bibi ducked against his stony side. Three dragons were heading in their direction. The smallest was being attacked by the bigger two; they snapped at his wings and tail, even though he begged them to stop.

'Combie... Mardie... stop it! You're hurting me!'

'Oooooooh! Poor little babeeeee! Who's an ickle pickle mummy's boy? Who's a mummy's pet?'

17

As the dragons circled over Bibi's head, the two larger dragons roared with laughter, and she was left coughing and spluttering thick smoke. Eyes streaming, throat burning, she jumped into the open and shook her fist.

'OI!' she shouted. 'Go away!' Snatching up a stone she hurled it at the biggest dragon. 'You're horrible bullies!'

There was an ear-piercing shriek and the dragon twisted in a spin.

'OW! OW! OW! Mummm*eeeeeeee*!' He and his brother hurtled off, the biggest wailing loudly.

Bibi's legs gave way, and she collapsed in a heap, wiping her smarting eyes. Dragons? Had she really seen dragons?

·˙✱·˙·

A sudden weight on her lap made her jump. The little dragon was lying beside her, his head on her knees. Bibi held her breath as she stared at his glittering body, and long dagger-like claws.

'Thank you,' he whispered. 'Combie and Mardie are terribly mean to me! Mama will be so cross when I tell her they were beastly to her ickle pickle Webster.' He rolled his silver eyes. 'Mama says I'm her ickle pickle precious pudding! Her cutie tootie pootie pie!'

Bibi was not impressed. But there was something she needed to know, so she did her best to smile.

'Why are you here? You haven't always lived in the valley, have you?'

Webster pouted. 'We had a lubbly wubbly cave... but there was a storm – a rumble – and a CRASH!!!

A monster rock rolled down the hill... and landed CRUNCH! In the doorway and shut us out!' He sniffed loudly. 'Mama says that's why we can't breathe fire. It's 'cos we can't get cosy warm at night.'

'So...' Bibi was trying not to sound excited. 'If the rock was taken away, would you go back?'

'YES!' Webster sat bolt upright. 'Can you move it?'

'I can't,' Bibi told him, 'but I know someone who can. Where's your cave?'

'Over the hill.' Webster pointed with a scaly foot. He jumped up and stretched his wings. 'I'll tell Mama!' And before Bibi could stop him, he was flapping across the valley, squeaking as he went. 'Mama! Mama! Your ickle pickle pudding has something lubbly wubbly to tell you!'

'Right!' Bibi took
a deep breath. The
boulder behind her was
unmoving. Marching over
to Glum she tapped him on
what she hoped was his back. 'Wake up,' she said. 'The
dragons have gone – and you're needed!'

There was a rumbling noise, and the giant's face
appeared.

'Is it safe?'

'Yes. I've made a discovery! The dragons are only
here because a huge rock has blocked their cave – so if
you move it, they'll go home! A great giant like you... it
should be easy peasy!'

Bibi waited for Glum to spring into action... but
he shook his head. 'Ever so EVER SO scary...' He was
already changing back into a boulder.

'Don't you see?' Bibi pleaded. 'You can have your
lovely valley back! There'll be no more clouds, no more
dust... and the sun will come out!'

But Glum was a boulder, solid and still.

'You're being STUPID!' Bibi shouted. Sylvestro
looked at her and shook his head.

'Don't do that,' Bibi said crossly. 'Can't you say anything helpful?' The cat got up, stretched, and sat down again. 'My old granny used to tell me, there's more than one way to tickle a trout. Why don't you try talking instead of shouting?'

'Because he won't listen!' Bibi snapped, and then it struck her. 'Tickling! Of course! That's how I woke him before!'

'That was not what my granny meant,' Sylvestro began, but Bibi was already trying to tickle Glum. There was a faint quiver, but the boulder was so rough her fingers felt sore.

I need something to tickle him with, she thought... and then she was running like the wind towards the fairies' house in the opening between the rocks.

'Hello!' she called, 'I need to borrow a broom. I've found a way to get rid of the dragons!'

There was a pause; then a window swung open, and a pale face with a pointed nose peered out. 'Brooms? What do you want our brooms for?'

'To tickle the giant!' Bibi clasped her hands together. 'If he can move the rock from the dragons' cave the dragons will leave... and the valley will be full of flowers! There won't be any more soot!'

The window was slammed shut.

I'm not going to cry, Bibi thought. *I'll find another way –*

CRASH! The front door burst open, and a crowd of fairies came bustling out. Some carried feather dusters, others snatched up their brooms.

'We're ready! Show us where to go!' They surrounded Bibi, laughing and chattering. 'We'll tickle the giant! We love tickling!' Their voices were like tinkling silver bells.

'Over here' Bibi said, and she was keeping her fingers crossed as she led them to Glum's side.

Soot and pebbles flew in all directions as the fairies set to work... but the boulder didn't stir.

'Please keep trying,' Bibi begged, and the fairies tickled until there was a quiver... and a shudder... and Glum sat up.

'Little lady,' he said, 'that tickles.'

'I'm sorry,' Bibi said, 'but you've got to help us!'

She turned to the fairies. 'If Glum helps he'll be the hero of the valley – isn't that right?'

'Yes! Yes! Yes!' The fairies waved their brooms and dusters. 'We'll ask you to tea! We'll cheer you every Tuesday! We'll build a statue! Whatever you want!'

Glum looked at them, and his craggy face cracked into a smile. 'Fairies? Are you talking to Glum? You never spoke before.'

Bibi couldn't stop herself. 'That's because you never talked to *them*! You were always hiding!'

Sylvestro raised an eyebrow, but said nothing.

Glum was still staring at the fairies. 'You'll invite me to tea? Me... Glum?'

'We will! We will!' Their voices were shrill like birds. 'Bring back the sun, and we'll give you honey cakes and jam!'

'Well...' Glum's smile widened. 'That does sound nice —'

WHIRRRRRRRRRRRRR

Soot swirled in the air as huge wings beat overhead. The fairies scattered, Glum sank into a boulder, Sylvestro hid behind him... and Bibi gulped.

This golden-scaled, scarlet-winged, steel-clawed dragon was far *far* bigger than Webster and his brothers. She circled once, then landed in a flurry of pebbles. She stepped forward and, to Bibi's astonishment, bowed her golden head.

'I understand,' she breathed, 'that you were kind to my precious son, Webster.'

'Oh...' Bibi wasn't sure what to do.

'And he tells me you can take away the rock that blocks our cave,' the dragon went on. 'Is this true?'

Bibi nodded. 'My friend can help.' She glanced at the boulder that was Glum. If it was possible for a boulder to look unenthusiastic, this one did.

The mother dragon bowed a second time. 'I would be happy to take your friend to my cave...'

'Oh! That would be wonderful! But... could you come back later?'

The dragon nodded. 'I will return soon.' Then, with a flash of menace, she added, 'Be careful not to waste my time.' With a sweep of her wings, she was gone.

'Oh dear.' Bibi turned to Sylvestro. 'I've got to make Glum go... how though? He's so scared!'

'I don't believe my wise old granny ever met a dragon,' the big black cat said. 'All the same... you could try talking to him? Not shouting. Talking.'

'It won't work for me.' Bibi shook her head.

'You don't know that,' Sylvestro told her. 'You haven't tried.'

Bibi shivered. This was her first quest... and she was going to fail.

'Glum.' She paused, thinking. 'I understand a little how you're feeling. If you don't talk to anybody, you feel safe... but you don't make friends. And if you're scared of something, it's easy to hide away. But look what you've done already... you've spoken to the fairies! They'll love you if you move the rock and help the dragons leave the valley... Please, Glum... please...'

She stopped. The lump in her throat was getting larger.

There was a rumble, a shaking of earth, and Glum

got slowly to his feet. Bibi gasped as he towered above her.

'Little lady,' he said, 'what do you want me to do?'

When the mother dragon returned, Glum and Bibi
were waiting for her. Bibi worried the giant might
change his mind, but he climbed onto the dragon's back
without a word. Bibi scrambled on behind him and
Sylvestro leaped onto the dragon's tail.

'This,' he remarked, 'is something my wise old granny has never ever done.'

As the scarlet wings spread wide, Bibi tightened her grip on Glum's stony jacket. They were flying! And as they flew, the regular wing beat steadied Bibi's fluttering heart. She looked down.

The soot-blackened valley was far below, and they were already over the hill. With a swoop and a swirl, the dragon dived down, and as the air rushed past, Bibi felt her fears blow away.

We might actually do it! she thought. *We might save the valley!*

·'*·,·

When the dragon landed, Sylvestro was the first to leap off. Glum stayed where he was, studying the rock blocking the cave.

'Is it too big?' Bibi whispered.

Glum chuckled. 'Too big, little lady?' He swung himself off the dragon's back, strode to the cave and

tossed the rock away, as if it weighed no more than an apple. 'There,' he said. 'All gone!'

The mother dragon bent her golden head to him.

'I will make you a promise. From now on, we will respect your right to the valley, and let you live in peace.' She turned to Bibi. 'Now our home is ours again we will sleep warm at night, and our fire will return. We may be of help on your quests. Should that day come, call for me.' She paused. 'You have shown me that my sons are in need of some correction. It will be seen to! First, I must reward you.' Furling her scarlet wings, she slipped into the cave.

'What does she mean?' Bibi asked.

Sylvestro shrugged. 'Wait and see.'

Even as he spoke, the mother dragon returned. 'Please accept this token of my thanks.' She held out something small and shiny. Bibi took it wonderingly… and found it was a key – a key engraved with dragons and flowers.

'Thank you! Thank you so SO much!' she said… but the dragon had gone.

Bibi looked at the key, her face glowing. 'Where should I keep it? It would be dreadful if I lost it…'

'Might I suggest my collar?' Sylvestro circled her legs. 'I believe Miss Myrtle asked me to wear it with that in mind.'

'Time to go, little lady.' Glum peered down at Bibi and Sylvestro, then stooped to offer them his hand. 'Allow me!' And the three of them set off, Bibi and the big black cat sitting high on Glum's shoulder.

'It's good to get moving again, little lady,' he said as they reached the top of the hill overlooking the valley. 'It's been a long time.'

Bibi didn't answer. When she had first seen the valley, it was blanketed in soot; now it was a vivid green... and as Glum strode nearer, she could see the fairies sweeping and cleaning. As they caught sight of the giant there was a twinkle of wings, and Bibi was surrounded by such a cloud of glitter that she was dazzled.

'Thank you, thank you, thank you!' The fairies sang in her ear.

'Indeed, little lady,' Glum said, as he gently lifted Bibi to the ground. 'I thank you too.'

'Come to tea! Come to tea!' the bell-like voices called. 'Honey cakes and jam, sugar and spice, sweet lemonade, marzipan...'

Bibi's stomach rumbled as she hurried after the fairies. To her surprise, the gap between the rocks was much larger. *I'll be able to fit through*, she thought happily.

'Enter! Enter!' The fairies fluttered round her.

And Bibi stepped through the door...

AN OAK, A PiNE,
AND AN APPLE TREE

ibi's eyes opened wide. In front of her was a tall
grey tower; Sylvestro was at her feet and she
looked at him, smiling. 'Do you think there's a
princess locked in there? Or a prince?'

The big black cat twirled a whisker. 'Who knows?
But there's someone in the garden.' He sniffed. 'They
seem to think they're singing, but I'm not sure I'd call it
that.'

The sound came from behind an old apple tree, and
Bibi hurried round to look. A girl in an orange dress
was sitting on the grass, drooping over a guitar. As Bibi
came closer, she could hear the words of her song.

'I cannot see you, brother fair
'Cos I am here and you are there
If you were here, oh brother sweet,
That would be a wonderful treat – no,
no, NO!'

The singer shook her head. 'What else rhymes with sweet?'

'Meat?' Bibi suggested, and the girl swung round.

'I can't possibly sing that! Who are you?'

'I'm Bibi.' Seeing the girl was wearing a crown, she asked, 'Are you a princess?'

The girl sighed. 'Princess Marissa.'

Bibi sat down beside her. 'Why are you here?'

Marissa sighed again. 'My brother, Prince Grandioso, is locked in that tower. My sisters were taking turns to sing to him so he'd know he wasn't forgotten... but one by one they've disappeared. They told me to stay at home because I'm the youngest. I'm

40

lonely on my own though, so I came too.' She looked at Bibi. 'You haven't seen my sisters, have you?'

'No.' Bibi was pleased her guess had been right. 'Who locked your brother up, Princess Marissa?'

'A wizard called Fractious. He's horribly evil.' Marissa shuddered. 'Grandioso told him he couldn't marry Suella – that's my oldest sister – and he flew into a dreadful rage. He waved his hands and – abracadabra! – Grandie was in the tower!'

'A real wizard?' Bibi hoped she didn't sound anxious.

'As real as they come.' Marissa picked up her guitar. 'I ought to start singing.'

Bibi stared at her. 'Why don't your parents send an army or something?'

Marissa shook her head. 'We're orphans. Grandioso looks after us.'

Bibi opened her mouth to ask why the sisters couldn't look after themselves, but decided against it. 'So why don't *you* rescue your brother?'

Marissa was horrified. 'And put him in danger? That wizard's powerful. They say he turns people into frogs, or rats, or mice, with one wave of his hand.'

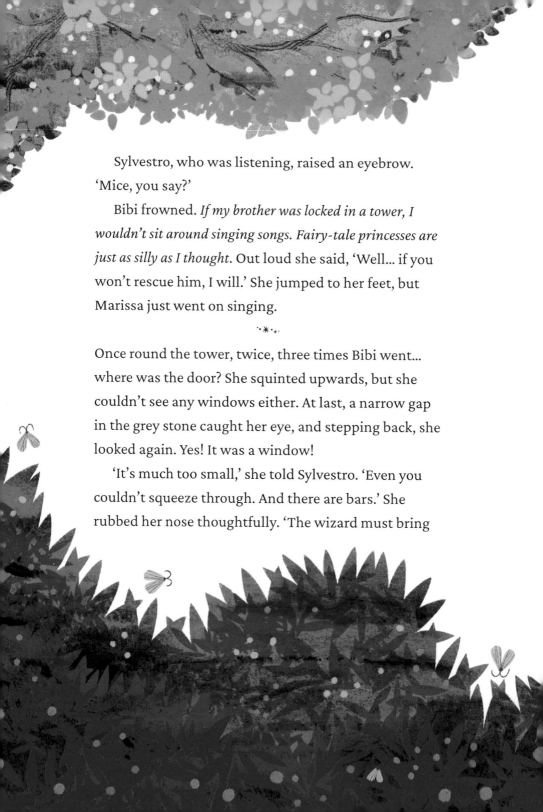

Sylvestro, who was listening, raised an eyebrow. 'Mice, you say?'

Bibi frowned. *If my brother was locked in a tower, I wouldn't sit around singing songs. Fairy-tale princesses are just as silly as I thought.* Out loud she said, 'Well... if you won't rescue him, I will.' She jumped to her feet, but Marissa just went on singing.

·.✳·.·

Once round the tower, twice, three times Bibi went... where was the door? She squinted upwards, but she couldn't see any windows either. At last, a narrow gap in the grey stone caught her eye, and stepping back, she looked again. Yes! It was a window!

'It's much too small,' she told Sylvestro. 'Even you couldn't squeeze through. And there are bars.' She rubbed her nose thoughtfully. 'The wizard must bring

the prince food and water. I'll stay and watch. When I see how he gets inside I'll learn how to do it too.'

They looked for somewhere to hide; a laurel bush offered a good view, and Bibi wriggled in among the thick leathery leaves. Sylvestro curled up and went to sleep.

·✳·✦·

It seemed like a long time before there was the sound of footsteps. Bibi carefully moved a branch to peer out. A stout figure was puffing towards her, carrying a basket. Could it be Fractious?

Bibi's heart missed a beat, and for a moment she wondered if she should leave the prince to his fate. The wizard was small, but there was a darkness about him; it was difficult to say what colour his long flowing beard was... Grey? Black? Or even green? His sharp eyes flickered from side to side, and Bibi froze in case a movement gave her away.

I can do this, she told herself. *I can... I know I can.*

As she watched, the wizard tapped on the tower wall.

CRACKLE! FLASH! ZAP!

A staircase appeared, winding round and round the walls like a helter-skelter at the fair. He climbed up. He passed the narrow window, reached the top... and disappeared.

Sylvestro had woken up and was watching the wizard. 'Could there be a door on the roof?'

'Sssh! I'm trying to remember which stone he tapped.' Step by cautious step, Bibi tiptoed to the tower. Picking up a stone she scratched a cross on the wall, then crept back to her hiding place. She was just in time: as she crouched down among the leaves the wizard came hurrying out. Once on the ground he snapped his fingers, and the staircase vanished. As he hurried away, Bibi found herself shivering.

Sylvestro's fur was standing on end. 'A nasty piece of work.'

Bibi agreed. There was something about the wizard that made her knees weak and her stomach churn...

but she was determined to rescue Grandioso. She unhooked the key from Sylvestro's collar. 'Do you think this might help?'

Sylvestro put his head on one side. 'You won't know unless you try. I'll stay here and keep watch.'

Bibi gave him a suspicious glance. 'You won't catch any mice, will you? They might be humans under the wizard's spell...'

'*HSSSSSST!*' The big black cat's whiskers bristled.

'I'm sorry,' Bibi told him. 'I forgot you're a fairy-tale cat.'

Sylvestro didn't answer. He began cleaning his paws and Bibi guessed she was forgiven. She waited to make sure Fractious had gone, then marched towards the tower.

'Here goes,' she said, and tapped the key on the stone.

CRACKLE! FLASH! ZAP!

The staircase appeared so suddenly Bibi had to jump out of the way. She scrambled up, but as she passed the window, a pale face pressed itself against the bars. An astonished voice asked, 'Who are you?'

'I've come to rescue you.' Bibi crossed her fingers. 'Is there a door in the roof?'

'Be careful!' the prince warned. 'Fractious has magic powers—'

His voice was cut off by a frantic squeaking.

'*Eeeeeeek! Eeeeeeeek!*'

'What's that noise?'

'I told you. The wizard has magic powers. He's turned six of my sisters into mice. You don't want to be a mouse as well, do you?'

Ignoring the butterflies in her stomach, Bibi stuck out her lower lip. 'I'm not going to get caught.' She went on climbing.

At the top of the staircase was a low parapet, hiding a turret on the roof. A wooden door showed her the way in.

And if I can get in, the prince can get out, she told herself. She glanced down to see if she could signal to Sylvestro... and gasped.

Fractious was hurrying back. His head was lowered, so it was possible he hadn't seen the staircase; Bibi, trembling, held the key tightly in one hand and snapped her fingers with the other.

Would it work?

She bit her lip...

YES! The staircase vanished as swiftly as it had appeared.

Bibi leaped down the steps into Grandioso's gloomy prison.

'Help! The wizard's coming! I've got to hide!'

'In here...' Grandioso pulled open a small cupboard door. 'Quickly!

Bibi squeezed inside, and Grandioso slammed the door shut. Left in pitch darkness, her heart beat so hard she was sure it would give her away.

'I have news for you.' The wizard's voice was a rasp. 'A seventh whiskered one will be joining you soon. The last of your sisters has come within reach of my powers.

Even now she is singing a dreary song to remind you that you are not forgotten! My spells are ready. She will be an easy catch.'

'Sir... how long will this go on?' Grandioso pleaded. 'Six of my sisters are here already, complete with tails and whiskers. They've done you no harm. It was I who offended you. Can't you find any kindness in yourself to let them go?'

'Kindness? To you, who stood in the way of my wishes?' The wizard sneered. 'Never! And once I have seven mousekins as my humble servants I'll fly away to my castle in the sky. Perhaps in time the lovely Suella will tire of her paws and her claws, and agree to be my wife.'

'And what will become of me, sir?' Grandioso asked.

'You will stay here for ever and ever—' Fractious paused. 'Unless you can break my spell.'

'How will I do that?'

'This is what you must do, you, who are locked away by flame and fire...

> *'Here in this tower, bring all three,*
> *An oak, a pine and an apple tree!*

'But my spells are strong. You will never overcome my magic powers, foolish prince.' And with a mocking cackle, Fractious stamped out of the room.

As his footsteps faded, Grandioso opened Bibi's tiny cupboard.

'Wow!' Bibi said. 'He's scary!'

The prince nodded. He was pale, and his six mice sisters were sitting in a row wiping their eyes. 'You'd better go, my friend. Don't risk him finding you.' He hesitated. 'He said my youngest sister's here. Did you see her? Can you warn her to escape?'

'I'll warn her,' Bibi promised, 'but why can't you leave? He didn't lock the door.'

'Don't you think I would if I could?' The prince's voice was sad. 'Watch.' He took a step towards the

door, then another – and WHOOOOOOOOSH!
Roaring flames flared, and the room was alive with
blazing light and dancing shadows. Grandioso leaped
backwards, rubbing at his tunic to put out a scatter of
sparks.

As the flames sank to nothingness, Bibi swallowed.
'I see.' She glanced at the row of mice. 'Is it the same for
your sisters?'

'The same.' Grandioso slumped against the wall.

'We're trapped. There's nothing you can do.'

Bibi frowned. 'I can still try. Your sister Marissa's outside. We can make a plan together.'

'A plan?' Grandioso shook his head wearily. 'To dig up three trees and haul them here? No. Just make certain that Marissa is safe.' And he turned away.

'Eeeeek?' The largest mouse came scuttling across the table. Sitting on her tail, she clapped her pink paws, then pointed to the doorway.

'You think I can do it?' Bibi asked, and the mouse clapped again. Bibi took the mouse's tiny paw in hers and shook it. 'I'll do my best. I promise.'

'Eeeeek.' The mouse twirled her tail, and she and her sister mice waved as Bibi walked uncertainly towards the door. Would the flames burn her too?

She heaved a sigh of relief as she stepped into the open air, but her mind was whirling. She had promised to help – but how?

I'll work something out, Bibi thought. *I have to! But first I have to get to the ground.*

She checked to make sure there was no sign of Fractious,

but all she could see was Sylvestro, prowling among the bushes.

'Sylvestro!' she called. 'Can you tap on the stone? The one with the cross?'

The cat did so... but nothing happened. Bibi's stomach clenched. 'I'll drop the key... can you try with that?'

CRACKLE! FLASH! ZAP!

The twisting stair wrapped around the tower and Bibi flew down the steps to find Marissa... but when she reached the spot where the princess had been, only her guitar lay on the grass, with a half-eaten apple.

'*Oh NO!*' Bibi stared in horror. She was too late. What had the wizard said? Once he had all seven sisters he was going to leave the tower and fly to his castle in the sky. How would she ever get there?

Think, Bibi... think! She stared at the guitar. *Marissa must have been caught by surprise... she didn't even have time to*

54

finish her apple...

Her apple!

The idea exploded in Bibi's head. 'I know what to do!' she shouted, then clamped her hand over her mouth. Had Fractious heard?

'You called?' Sylvestro appeared on silent velvet paws.

'I can save them!' Bibi stuffed the apple into her pocket. 'But I need to find two more trees, an oak, and a pine, before Fractious comes back!'

She spun round, scanning the woods by the tower.

'Oh! A pine tree! I need a pine cone...'

'Merrrrrow!' Sylvestro leaped into the branches and knocked a cone off its twig. Bibi snatched it up. 'Thank you!' she called.

And now to find an oak.

This way and that she ran...
a beech. A birch. A plum...
and there it was. An oak
tree! Acorns lay scattered

in the grass, and with a cry of delight Bibi pushed a handful in her other pocket. Then, heart pounding, she rushed to the tower.

The stairs were still there... and halfway up, Marissa slung over his shoulder, was Fractious. Bibi froze. The wizard was climbing steadily. Another six or seven steps and he would be through the turret door.

Gritting her teeth, Bibi scrambled after him, expecting to be blasted with a spell at any second – and reached the parapet as the door closed.

It's now or never, she thought. Holding her breath she turned the handle, wincing at the tiny click... and crept down the steps.

·*·*·

Fractious was in the middle of the tower room and in front of him, hardly able to stand, was Marissa. Grandioso had his arm round her, and the six little mice were cowering in a corner.

'So now,' the wizard growled, 'as the seventh sister stands before you, my plan is complete. All that remains...' he pointed a clawed finger at Marissa, 'is to cast the final spell—'

'Wait!' Bibi shouted.

The wizard swung round, and she held out her hands.
'Look—

    'Here to the tower, I bring all three
    An oak, a pine and an apple tree...'

And she dropped an acorn, a pine cone and an apple pip at the wizard's feet.

ſiLENCE... Bibi tingled all over.

Had she got it right? Was it going to work?

With a mighty howl that shook the walls, the wizard flung up his arms... and the room was filled with swirling mist and a thousand glittering stars. They were so bright that Bibi shut her eyes. When she looked again, all that was left was a heap of crumpled clothes. Six tall girls were hugging Marissa and Grandioso as if they would never let them go... and then Bibi too was hugged and thanked over and over again.

'You saved us,' Grandioso told her. 'Saved us from a terrible fate...'

Bibi couldn't answer; all she could do was point. The acorn, the pine cone and the apple pip had sunk deep into the floor, and green shoots were leaping upwards. The stone walls were melting away on either side, and a soft summer breeze ruffled her hair. Grandioso and his sisters held her hands and laughed.

As Bibi looked round in wonder, she saw the tower was nothing more than a circle of mossy stones. In the centre, three young trees lifted

their branches to the sky... an oak, a pine and an apple tree.

'Come with us to our palace,' Marissa begged. 'We'll dress you in silks and satins, and celebrate with a feast!' She giggled. 'I'll make up a new song telling the world how you defeated the evil wizard!'

Bibi hesitated. *I've never been to a palace... or worn silks and satins...* but then she thought of her mum, and Miss Myrtle and the magic box.

'I have to go,' she said as she saw Sylvestro beckoning to her from high up on a branch. 'I'm sorry...'

Grandioso bowed, and his sisters curtsied.

'Before you leave us,' the prince said, 'may we offer you this, by way of thanks?' He held out a key decorated with a mouse.

Bibi's hand shook with excitement as she took it. She had earned her second key...

'Thank you! Thank you!'

Then, with a wave, she scrambled up the tree to join the big black cat.

THE MAGIC PEBBLE

'Wooooo!' Bibi's hair blew into her eyes as she stepped onto the sand, and for a moment she couldn't see. The wind was clean and fresh, and a seagull was calling Keeeow! Keeeow! Keeeow! She looked around in wonder.

White-tipped waves danced over the sea, and rock pools gleamed like so many little mirrors. Bibi longed to run and see if they were full of secret treasures, but Sylvestro was disapproving.

'Far too much water for my liking.' The big black cat shook the sand off his paws. 'And I rather think I can see smoke...'

Sylvestro was right. Pulling off her shoes, Bibi ran along the beach towards a wisp of smoke curling up

from behind a heap of tumbled rocks. Sylvestro sighed
and followed her.

It was a very small house with a very small garden,
and a very small man was sorting shells on the step.
When he saw Bibi he rushed into his house, slamming
the door behind him.

'Oh dear,' Bibi said. 'He looked terrified!'

'Wouldn't you be if you met someone twice your
size?' Sylvestro asked.

Bibi was looking round. 'I love this... it's a shell
garden!' She squatted down to look closer. 'Oh no!

Here's a bit that's been spoiled. Let's see... I think I can put it back together.' Carefully she gathered up the scattered shells and arranged them to fit the pattern. 'Is that right?'

Before Sylvestro could answer, the front door flew open and a very small woman rushed out. She was carrying a rolling pin, and she shook it furiously at Bibi.

'Be off with you! Haven't you caused enough trouble? Go away! Go away now!'

Bibi stared at her. 'I haven't done anything!'

'Don't give me that!' The very small woman was purple with rage. 'You water sprites are all the same! Spoiling my Humbert's garden— *Oh!*'

Her expression changed so suddenly that Bibi almost laughed.

'Oh, oh, *oh!* You've mended it!'

Bibi nodded. 'It's ever so pretty.'

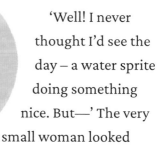

'Well! I never thought I'd see the day – a water sprite doing something nice. But—' The very small woman looked puzzled. 'Where's your tail?'

'I haven't got a tail.' Bibi was half amused, half irritated. 'And I'm not a water sprite. I don't even know what that is.'

'Trouble. That's what.' The rolling pin was shaken under Bibi's nose. 'They come sneaking up here to steal our shells, leaving nothing but mess, and froggy footprints.' She bent down to stare at Bibi's bare feet. 'H'm! You're right. You aren't a sprite. You've not got froggy feet.' She turned, shouting in a surprisingly loud voice for such a little person, 'HUMBERT!'

As the very small man came hurrying out, his wife pointed to Bibi. 'She's mended your pattern!'

Humbert's eyebrows shot up. 'A water sprite?'

'She's not.' His wife gave Bibi a questioning look. 'Seeing as you're the helpful type, suppose you help some more?'

70

'What with?' Bibi was cautious, and the very small woman put her hands on her hips.

'Not so helpful now, eh? Not when it means a bit of hard work.'

'I've never been afraid of hard work,' Bibi said indignantly. 'What do you want me to do?'

'Stop those water sprites spoiling our garden. They've no business bothering us sea elves. It's making my Humbert unhappy.' The very small woman looked so fondly at her husband that Bibi's irritation melted away. 'It's wearing him out...' And she wiped a tear with a corner of her apron.

'I'll try,' Bibi told her, 'although I don't know what water sprites are, or where I'd find them.'

'In the sea, of course. Related to fairies, but far more tricksy. Here!' The very small woman fished in her pocket and pulled out a rough brown pebble with a hole in the centre. 'Take this. It might help...'

As Bibi took the gift, her hand tingled. 'What does it do?'

'Remember this: *Pibble pebble, pobble pebble, make me small!* And when you want to be full size again, say, *Pobble pebble, pibble pebble, make me tall.*' The very small woman gave Bibi a brisk nod. 'Can you remember that?'

'*Pibble pebble, pobble pebble, make me small!*' Bibi repeated... and she had the most peculiar feeling. There was a roaring in her ears, and she was shrinking – DOWN, DOWN, DOWN. Just as she was beginning to wonder if she would disappear altogether, she stopped... and found herself staring up at the very small woman, who now seemed enormous.

'Help!' Bibi squeaked.

'Remember the words!' The voice echoed high above.

'Oh yes...' Bibi clutched the charm in her hand. '*Pobble pebble, pibble pebble, make me tall!*'

There was a WHOOOOOOSH and a breathless Bibi shot up to her normal size. 'Wow! That was so *weird*!'

'There's one more thing.' The very small woman waved her rolling pin. 'Don't EVER use it to make yourself bigger than you are! You'll be in real trouble if you do. But you'd better get going. If you want to find the water sprites, look through the hole.' She linked

her arm through her husband's. 'You can come and tell us when you're done. We'll thank you then.' And she and Humbert trotted back into their very small house, shutting the door behind them.

'I suppose that must be my quest.' Bibi looked at Sylvestro, who was curled up on the roof looking like a furry tea cosy. 'Have you ever met a water sprite?'

The cat shook his head. 'Never.' He stretched and stood up. 'You won't have seen one because you're human. Look through the hole in the stone.'

Bibi put the pebble to her eye – and gasped. Skipping in and out of the waves as they rippled to the shore were two girls carrying baskets – one tall, and one about Bibi's height. Their dresses floated around them, and their hair twisted in curly tendrils; only their long green tails and webbed feet proved they weren't human.

'WOW! I can actually see them!' Bibi put the pebble down. 'And I still can!'

'Be careful!' Sylvestro warned. 'Once they realise you can see them, they'll want to know why.'

Sylvestro was right. The smaller water sprite was staring at Bibi.

'Can you really see me?' she asked. Bibi nodded, and the sprite came nearer. 'But aren't you a human?'

'Yes,' Bibi said, 'and I'm on a quest. Is it you that steals the shells from Humbert's garden?'

The sprite gave her companion a sideways glance and edged closer. 'I know it's mean – but it's my cousin, Gull. She gets cross if she doesn't collect enough. The Sea King is building a shell grotto, you see. There's a competition: us water sprites have to collect shells, and he gives out pearls as prizes. Today it's a beautiful pink pearl necklace, and Gull's desperate to win it—'

'Mer! What *are* you doing?' Mer's cousin glared at her. 'That's a *human*!'

Mer hung her head. 'I'm sorry, Gull... but she can see us...'

'She can?' Gull turned to Bibi, her green eyes sharp. 'Is that right, human girl?'

'Yes.' Bibi had taken an instant dislike to Gull. 'I was asking Mer why you steal Humbert's shells.'

'Why does it matter?' the sprite demanded. 'He's only a silly little sea elf. He can go to Sweetwater Bay and collect as many shells as he wants. It's not far.'

Bibi's eyes flashed. 'If it's so near, why don't *you* go there to collect shells?'

But Gull had had enough. She grabbed Mer's arm and dragged her away. 'Ignore the human,' she ordered. 'I need to fill my basket.' And she led her cousin up the beach to Humbert's precious garden.

'*Hey,*' Bibi shouted. She was about to rush after them when a thought made her stop. *Who was it that Mer had mentioned? The Sea King?* She rubbed her nose. *I need to find out more...*

Fingering the stone in her pocket, she

tried to work out a plan. *What if I go back with them to wherever they live? But it'll be in the sea!* She glanced round and found Sylvestro beside her. 'I'm not good at swimming,' she told him. 'But I want to follow them...'

'You've got the magic pebble, haven't you?' The cat twirled a whisker. 'You'll find you can breathe as easily underwater as on land. Just don't expect me to come with you.'

'Oh, I won't,' Bibi promised. She turned the stone a second time as she watched Gull stamping through the garden, picking up the prettiest shells and ruining the patterns that Bibi had so carefully put back in place.

Am I brave enough?

As if in answer, Humbert's tear-streaked face

appeared at the window of his house, and she made up her mind. *I'll do it!*

Gull was the nearest, and her basket was on the ground. Holding the stone tightly, Bibi murmured, '*Pibble pebble, pobble pebble, make me small!*'

Even though she was ready for the roaring noise, it was still a shock. And, worse still, the sand now felt like broken glass. She wished she had kept her shoes on; by the time she reached the basket her feet were stinging. Climbing up was easy, however, and she slipped over the basket's edge. A large cowrie shell offered the perfect hiding place, and she crept inside.

She was only just in time. Gull was ordering Mer to hurry; the basket was picked up, and Bibi was bumped and jolted as they ran down to the sea.

Even though Sylvestro had promised she would be safe, Bibi couldn't stop worrying as the water swirled around her. Shutting her eyes tightly, she held her breath, and counted slowly as the water sprites swam down, down, down into the secret depths of the ocean.

There was a jolt, and a thump as the basket was dumped on a rock... and she opened her eyes to find she was underwater, breathing normally. Relief made her brave, and she inched out from her shell, only to scuttle straight back in. Gull was right beside her.

'Look at these shells! I'm sure to win the pink pearl necklace!' Gull sounded pleased with herself. 'I collected *loads* from that stupid old garden. It's *so* much easier than swimming to Sweetwater Bay, like the other water sprites. Mer—' She snapped her fingers. 'Carry my basket. It's time to show the king!'

Crouching inside, Bibi grew angrier and angrier. Gull had been cheating; she didn't deserve anything, let alone a reward... and she ordered Mer around as if she was her servant.

'Oooooch!' Bibi stifled a sneeze. Mer was bending over the basket, her long curly hair tickling Bibi's nose. Seizing the opportunity, Bibi swung herself up to hide on the water sprite's shoulder. Mer, unaware, picked up the basket and followed her cousin.

It was the ideal hiding place; Bibi's eyes widened as she saw they were in an underwater cavern. Two of the walls were decorated with lines of gleaming shells, but the third wall was unfinished. *So that's what the shells are for*, she thought.

In the centre of the cavern was an enormous throne, glittering with sea glass, and a tall figure leaned on a golden trident. His robes rippled and swirled around him, and his hair was emerald green beneath a golden crown. A crowd of water sprites stood near, each carrying a basket.

'Thank you, my dears!' The Sea King's deep voice rumbled round the walls. 'You have been busy! Tell me, was Sweetwater Bay kind to you?'

There was a chorus of agreement. Bibi clenched her fists when she saw Gull joining in; only Mer bit her lip and was silent.

'Show me what you have brought,' the king said, and he sat back on his throne. 'If we have enough shells to complete our grotto, you will all be rewarded!'

'But Your Majesty – what about the prize?' It was Gull, and her voice was anxious.

The king smiled and held up a necklace. The pink pearls glimmered in the pale light, and there was a murmur of excitement. 'This, my dears,' the king said, 'will be my gift to the sprite who has collected the most shells today.'

As the sprites presented their baskets, Gull moved to the back of the line, pulling Mer with her.

'If he asks where we've been, make sure you say Sweetwater Bay!' she hissed. 'But that's a lie,' Mer protested. 'Ouch!' Gull had pinched her.

'It's not *really* a lie.' Bibi could feel Gull's breath as the sprite crouched beside her cousin. 'The sea elf collected them from Sweetwater Bay, didn't he? So that's where they came from!'

There wasn't time for Mer to answer. The line of water sprites had moved forward, and it was Gull's turn to hold out her basket. The Sea King took it with an approving nod.

'A wonderful collection,' he said, and Gull simpered. 'I did my best, Your Majesty.'

The king picked up a speckled cockle shell. 'I've never seen one like this before. Where did you find it?'

Gull blinked. After the tiniest pause, she said, 'Near

the cliff, Your Majesty.' She turned to Mer. 'Isn't that right?'

Bibi had heard enough. 'Say *no*!' she whispered in Mer's ear. 'Say *no*!'

Mer's squeal of surprise was so loud that Gull dropped her basket, and the Sea King raised his eyebrows.

'Is something troubling you?' he asked.

'She said yes.' Gull glared at her cousin. 'Didn't you, Mer?'

'Don't listen to her!' Bibi urged. 'Tell the truth!'

Mer opened and closed her mouth, but said nothing.

Bibi tweaked her hair. 'If you let her, she'll bully you forever!'

'Ummm.' Mer stepped away from Gull, twisting her fingers together. 'I don't exactly know... that is...'

She swallowed hard, and her words came in a rush.

85

'The shells are from a garden, Your Majesty – a sea elf's garden – and I'm very sorry, because it made him sad!'

The Sea King was no longer smiling as he looked at Gull. 'Is this true?'

'NO!' Gull stamped her foot. 'She's telling lies! She's jealous because I'm older and cleverer!'

The king stroked his chin as he studied first Gull, then Mer. 'So, who should I believe?'

It was time for action. Bibi slid off Mer's shoulder, and half fell, half scrambled to the sandy floor, muttering, '*Pobble pebble, pibble pebble – make me tall!*'

WHOOOOOOOOOOOOOOOSH!

The water sprites shrieked as Bibi burst into being, and the Sea King leaped to his feet, trident at the ready.

'It's the human!' Gull gasped, and Mer stared in astonishment.

The king put down his weapon. 'A human child, here?'

86

Bibi, unsure how to greet a king, bowed. 'Excuse me, Your Majesty, but it's true. These shells come from Mr Humbert's garden... and he's very upset.' She put her arm round Mer. 'Mer didn't want to take them. Please don't be cross with her.'

The Sea King sighed. 'I want my people, water sprites and sea elves, to live in peace. It upsets me that one of my sprites has been selfish and unkind... but I have a solution. You' – he pointed at Gull, who wriggled uncomfortably – 'will take the shells back to Mr Humbert's garden. And you' – he pointed to Mer – 'may stay here... and be glad that you spoke the truth.' He turned to Bibi. 'Will you accompany Gull, human child, and see that all is done according to my wishes?'

Bibi beamed. 'Yes! Oh, thank you! Mr Humbert will be happy – and so will his wife!'

'Then let it be done...' And the Sea King held up his hand to show that the matter was settled.

🐈

When Humbert and his wife opened the door, Bibi showed them the basket of shells, and they danced her round and round until she was breathless.

'So, no more water sprites ruining my garden!' Humbert said, and he gave Gull a fierce look.

Gull hung her head. 'I promise... and... I'm sorry.'

As Gull trailed away to the sea, Humbert's very small wife pulled at Bibi's arm.

'Here's a present for you, human child,' she said, 'to thank you.' She handed Bibi a small key covered in tiny shells. 'But now it's time for you to go. That big black cat of yours is curled up waiting.' And before Bibi could thank her, she took Humbert's hand and bustled him away.

Sylvestro sprang down from the roof of the house. He purred loudly as Bibi added the key to his collar and she smiled. 'So, where do we go now?'

The cat twirled a whisker. 'I'd say that cave looks promising...'

Bibi turned to look. She was sure a cave hadn't been there before... and she gave a skip of excitement as she led the way towards her next quest.

AN ENCHANTED GARDEN

ibi stepped into the garden. It was so beautiful that she didn't know where to look first; blue delphiniums echoed the sky, snow-white lilies opened their hearts to the sunshine, and crimson peonies tossed their petals on the twisting path. Trees hung heavy with apples and pears, and bent under the weight of ripe plums.

'Wow...' Bibi twirled round in excitement. 'Don't you think it's lovely?'

The big cat shivered. 'There's something peculiar going on,' he said. 'I can feel it in my whiskers.'

'Could I take some fruit home to Mum? What do you think?' Bibi stretched a hand to pick an apple... and the branch swept out of reach.

She blinked. There was no wind, so what had happened? She turned to a pear tree, and tried again. There was the swish of leaves – and the pear was high above her head.

'As I thought.' Sylvestro sounded smug. 'It's all too good to be true.'

Bibi bent down to pick a rose and was met with a sharp thorn. 'Ouch! You're right,' she said. 'It might look lovely, but it's not exactly welcoming. What kind of quest is this?'

Sylvestro shrugged. 'That's for you to find out.'

Bibi glanced at the rose. 'That was mean. My thumb really hurts!'

Sylvestro didn't answer, and Bibi suddenly noticed how very quiet it was. No birds were singing, and no bees or butterflies danced among the flowers.

'It's weird... I can't hear anything,' she said, and then, 'Oh! What's that?'

Sylvestro's ears twitched. 'Voices. Squeaky ones.'

He was right. Bibi could hear the sound of distant chatter...

'Let's find them!'

Bibi hurried along the path. It twisted and turned

and curled back on itself, but a final corkscrew bend took her through a rose arch and into a strangely empty space. Instead of grass there was bare earth, and in front of her was a group of curious little creatures – mothers, fathers, children and a few aged grandmothers. They were on their knees digging, as if searching for something precious, and they were too busy to notice Bibi.

Were they gnomes? Or goblins? They had large, pointed ears and greenish faces, and their feet were wide and flat.

'Gnomes.' Sylvestro had read her thoughts. 'Mostly harmless, and not very clever.' He yawned, and strolled a little way away; yawning again, he chose a shady spot and curled up. 'Time for a cat nap,' he remarked, and closed his eyes.

'That's all very well,' Bibi said, 'but what am I supposed to do?' Hearing her voice, one of the little gnomes looked up.

'*EEEEEEEEEK!*' he yelled, and he hid in his mother's skirts. The other gnomes jumped to their feet, waving their spades threateningly, and the babies began to cry.

'Go way, giant!' An old gnome scowled at Bibi. 'Go way!'

Bibi kneeled down so she was closer to the gnome's height. 'I'm not a giant,' she said, 'and I promise I won't hurt you!'

'You say no hurty,' the gnome said. 'How we know you speak truly true?'

Bibi rubbed her nose. 'What would make you believe me?'

The gnome considered. 'Help Biddle find spangle stones.'

'Who's Biddle?' Bibi asked. 'And what are spangle stones?'

'I is Biddle!' The old gnome put her hands on her hips. 'You not see I is Biddle? Biddle is toppest gnome! Head gardener! And spangle stones…' she pointed to her throat, 'spangle stones is twinkly-winkly, neck-pretty.'

'Do you mean a necklace?' Bibi guessed, and Biddle scowled again.

'I did say so! Neck-pretty! You is dippy. You no help.' And she turned to the other gnomes.

'I'm sorry,' Bibi said. 'I just didn't understand. But who does the necklace – I mean, neck-pretty – belong to?'

'Who you think? Us! Is our treasure... But airy fairy – she has hid it!' Biddle tossed the information over her shoulder, and Bibi felt a spark of excitement. She wanted to know more, but Biddle was shooing her family and friends back to work, digging and sieving the earth. As Bibi watched, she saw that as soon as they reached one side of the patch they turned round and went back again.

That's so weird, she thought.

Biddle seemed to be ignoring her, so Bibi settled herself beside a grandfather.

'Please,' she said, 'why are you looking for the necklace here?'

The grandfather didn't answer; it was a small boy gnome who said, 'He am deaf. Here is where we looks for neck-pretty; here is where magic words does tell us to.' And he pointed to the rock that marked the end of the patch. Curious, Bibi went to look. The rock was covered in scratchy writing; peering closely, she read out loud:

FEET IN EARTH
HEAD IN SKY
STRETCHING ARMS
REACHING HIGH
CIRCLES, CIRCLES,
ROUND AND ROUND
WHAT IS HIDDEN
CAN BE FOUND.

'See?' The boy gnome stretched out a muddy foot. 'Feet in earth. And we goes round and round, like telling says.' He beamed at Bibi. 'One days we find spangle stones and then – *wheeeeeeeee!!!*' His face glowed. 'Then we has all flowery boweries and fruities and green lovelies back again!'

'I tried to pick an apple,' Bibi said, 'but the tree wouldn't let me.'

The boy gnome nodded. 'Fruities taken away by fairy. But her did promise. When we finding spangle stones, her not cross no more. When her think us goody goody and not nasty naughties, we can have all apples and pears!'

'Nasty naughties?' Bibi was surprised.

The boy gnome looked to left and right, then whispered, 'Sssh! Open ear holes, and I tell you. Us was goody goody garden workers... us growed pretty floweries for our fairy. But...' He gave a sigh. 'Was roundy roundy big moon time. Airy fairies dance at big moon, and fly high high high... but gnomies, we do always sleep so not see, not know. This night, baby was cry cry cry; we was awake! Never seen airy fairy fly high with her friendies... so we think big birds come to

steal apples and pears! We not look proper.' The boy
gnome shook his head sadly. 'We throw sticks.' There
was a heavier sigh. 'Fairy not hurt... but she angry angry
angry. She say, we must learn lesson... she hid spangle
stones. Now we must find... or no garden. Not never.'
And he wiped away a tear.

'I'm so sorry,' Bibi said. 'It sounds like a harsh punishment. You were only trying to protect the garden.'

The boy gnome's face lit up. 'We find spangle stones – then all is better! All is good good goodest and – OW! Ear hurty, Biddle! Ear hurty!'

'Here is work, not chatter chatter chat!' Biddle had tweaked the boy gnome's ear and was glaring at Bibi. 'You talk muchly too much, Snubs! You is useless gnome!'

Snubs hung his head. 'I not useless...'

'Yes you is.' Biddle tweaked his ear again. 'Was
you did throw sticks at airy fairy. I did see! You is bad
rotten egg gnome. You good for nothing! Go work with
others!'

Tears rolled down Snubs's cheeks, and he sobbed as
he trailed away, dragging his little spade behind him.

Bibi caught Biddle's arm. 'Don't be cross with him.
It was my fault he wasn't working. I wanted to know
about the garden.' She pointed to the rock. 'Was it the
fairy who gave that clue?'

For a moment she thought Biddle wasn't going to
answer; she still looked angry.

'Of course was airy fairy.' The gnome folded her
arms. 'Who else? And we will find our precious spangle
stones; we hard workers. We always keeping footsies
in the earth. We always going round and round and
round! And when we do find—' her frown faded '—us
will dance and sing and party all day long!'

Bibi looked at the rock again. 'What about the
stretching arms?'

There was a snort. 'We does stretching! Lots and lots
of stretching! We is *always* stretching!'

'I was wondering if it was some kind of riddle,' Bibi

said soothingly. 'You know, like *What is always running, but always stays in the same place?'*

The gnome looked blank. 'I not understand.'

'Easy! A river!' Bibi waited for Biddle to laugh, but the old gnome shook her head.

'Rivers has no footsies.' She sniffed. 'Not do running. Stupid giant – you is dippy dippy dippy.' And she turned away.

Oh dear, Bibi thought. *They don't understand jokes. But I'm sure there's another answer to that rhyme... and I'm good at solving riddles.*

She wandered away to where Sylvestro lay sleeping. Periwinkles twinkled like blue stars, and snow-white daisies shone in the lush green grass.

'Found your quest?' The big black cat opened an eye.

'The gnomes are looking for their necklace,' Bibi told him. 'There's a clue written on a rock, and I think it's a riddle. Listen...

'Feet in earth,
Head in sky
Stretching arms,
Reaching high
Circles, circles,
Round and round
What is hidden
Can be found.'

'Certainly sounds like a riddle,' Sylvestro agreed.

'I'm going to solve it. I'm sure the answer is in the garden,' and Bibi set off down the path. Sylvestro stretched and followed her.

·*·

Like Sylvestro's soft padded paws, Bibi's feet made no sound. The silence was so loud she began to hum, to remind herself she was real. Occasionally a tree would sweep up its branches as she passed, as if wanting nothing to do with her, and the rustle of leaves was sudden and shocking.

It's creepy, Bibi thought, *like a ghost garden...* and she shivered, even though the sun was shining. She tried to think of something cheerful, but all that came to mind was Snubs as he walked away in tears.

Poor little gnome. She frowned as she remembered Biddle's treatment of him. *Snubs was only talking to me, and even if he did throw sticks at the fairy, it was for a good reason. It would serve Biddle right if it was Snubs who found the – what did he call it? The neck-pretty. But I'm sure it can't be in that patch of earth. They surely would have found it by now.*

Bibi stopped as a thought came to her, and Sylvestro raised his eyebrows. 'Had an idea?'

'Yes!' Bibi's eyes shone. 'If I found the necklace, I could take it to the gnomes... and make it look as if Snubs discovered it!' She gave a skip of excitement. 'What do you think?'

'Is your aim to help the gnomes, or to prove Biddle wrong?' Sylvestro looked at her.

Bibi blushed. 'Both,' she said, and the cat nodded. 'Delightfully honest. Do as you think best.'

· ✳ ·

The path took Bibi past all kinds of trees and bushes. She paused to study the tallest sunflowers, larkspurs and roses, and any other plant that reached to the sky, but found nothing.

Bibi was beginning to wonder if she was wrong about the riddle when the path took yet another twist, and she found herself in front of a low wall. Inside the wall was a circle of stones, and in the middle of the stones was a peach tree so heavy

110

with fruit that its branches
almost touched the ground.
Bibi's stomach rumbled, and she
climbed over the wall to look more
closely. The sun-warmed peaches
were flushed pink, and each one was a
perfect globe.

'Wow,' she breathed. 'They're beautiful...'

'*Round and round...*' The words of the riddle echoed
in her mind.

I'm in a circle, she thought, *and the circle is in a circle...
and the peaches are as round as round could be.*

Her heart began to beat faster as she stood on tiptoe.
Was something glittering? She couldn't be sure; the
leaves were so glossy that each one caught the light and
mirrored it back to the sun.

She went closer; the lowest branch was within reach
and she swung herself up and began to climb. Twigs
scratched her arms and caught her hair, and as she
scrambled higher the branches grew closer together.
She was forced to wriggle in between, and twice her
clothes were snagged and torn... but at last she reached
the top.

Bibi looked round, and there, beside her, was a sparkle brighter than any raindrop. Hardly able to believe her eyes, she picked up the necklace, and let out a whoop of joy. She slipped it into her pocket and, as she did so, a peach fell off the tree with a soft thud.

Oooops! She bit her lip. *The magic spell must be fading... I'd better hurry, or the gnomes might guess I've found the necklace.* She scrambled down the tree, and this time the branches parted to let her pass.

As Bibi flew in between the flowers it felt as if she would never reach the gnomes. Faster and faster she ran; she *had* to reach them before the spell was broken. On either side, flowers were regaining their scent, and when she saw a bumblebee hovering over a rose bush she wondered if she was already too late.

At last she came to the final twist of the path. Panting, she took the necklace out of her pocket, and scooped up a handful of earth. Carefully she muddied the necklace until its glitter was gone and put it in her pocket. Brushing the mud off her hands, she paused to steady her breathing... and walked through the rose arch to where the gnomes were digging and sieving, digging and sieving.

Snubs, in disgrace, was at the end of the line. Tears streaked his little face, and he shook his head as Bibi kneeled beside him.

'I not talk,' he whispered, 'or Biddle tweak ears!'

'I came to say I'm sorry I got you into trouble,' Bibi told him.

'Go way,' Snubs begged, and he began to dig at twice his normal speed. 'Go way from no-good gnome...'

Bibi took a deep breath. It was time to put her plan into action.

·*·

'LOOK!' She pointed to the opposite end of the patch. As the gnomes swivelled to see, she dropped the necklace by Snubs's spade and scuffed earth over it with her shoe.

'We see nothing.' Biddle frowned. 'You spoil our workings! We no like you, giant.'

Bibi moved towards the path. 'I thought I saw a bird,' she said. 'I'm sorry. I only came to say goodbye—'

'OOOOOOOOOOOOOOOOH!'

Snubs's shriek made everyone jump. Then he was running in circles, the necklace clutched in his muddy fist. 'I founded it! I founded the spangle stones!'

There was a stunned silence, followed by an ear-splitting roar.

114

'Three cheers for Snubs!' Bibi called, 'Hip! Hip! Hurrah!'

Biddle swung round with a sneer. 'See, giant? Was no silly dippy riddle. Feet in earth did do it! Did tell you!' And she stuck out her tongue. 'GAH!'

If Biddle hadn't put an arm round Snubs and given him a hug, Bibi would have told her what she thought. It was with some difficulty that she managed, 'Yes. You were quite right.'

'Airy fairy will say we is goodie good now!' Snubs wriggled away from Biddle and went on dancing his victory dance. 'When she come?'

'I'm here.'

The voice was so close that Bibi could feel a faint breath on her ear... but there was only a butterfly fluttering round her head. 'Where are you?' she asked.

'Here!' And she was pinched.

'Ouch!' Bibi rubbed her arm, and there was a delighted chuckle.

'Now you know I'm real!'

'You didn't need to pinch me,' Bibi complained, and there was another chuckle.

'What fun you humans are!' The voice dropped to a hushed whisper. 'And so clever. My darling little Snubs has learned not to throw sticks at me, and I have returned their necklace. So satisfying! And one more thing...' Bibi jumped as a key was pressed into her hand.

'There! But now...' – the voice grew loud – 'it's time for the celebrations to begin!'

And, where the butterfly had been circling, a fairy appeared. The gnomes gave a cheer and rushed towards her, carrying Snubs on their shoulders.

'Airy fairy! Airy fairy! We is goodie good gnomies now! We founded our twinkle-winkle neck-pretty!'

The fairy laughed and held out her arms. 'Well done, my lovelies! Well done!'

Sylvestro nudged Bibi. 'Time to go.'

Bibi was studying the key she had been given. 'Look!' she said. 'It's decorated with butterflies!' And, as they walked away, she looked over her shoulder to see the gnomes one last time. Snubs was in the centre of the circle with the airy fairy, and his little face was alight with happiness.

Pleased, Bibi headed towards the rose archway... and stopped. There was no garden on the other side... there was nothing. Nothing, but thick white mist...

UNiCoRN PiE

B ibi seemed to have stepped into a cloud. All she could see was white; only the solid ground beneath her feet told her she wasn't floating in the sky.

'Sylvestro?' she called. 'Are you there? I can't see you!'

The tip of a black tail steered towards her, and the big cat loomed out of the mist. His whiskers were jewelled with dew drops and his fur was damp.

'Most unpleasant.' And he sneezed, '*Atchoo!*'

'Where are we?' Bibi asked.

'No idea. I can only just see my toes.'

The mist lifted enough for Bibi to discover that she was on a hill. On the far side of the valley was a rocky

crag, and there, tossing its flowing mane, was a snow-white horse. Or was it? Pale light glinted on a silver horn... and then the mist swirled, and it vanished from view.

'A unicorn!' Bibi's eyes were wide as she glanced at Sylvestro. 'Did you see? A real live unicorn!'

Sylvestro was busy cleaning his paws. 'Anything's possible here.'

Bibi glowed with excitement. 'But I never believed in unicorns! I hope my quest is to find it... OH!' She froze. 'What's that?'

TAN TARA! TAN TARA! TAN TARA!

Hunting horns echoed across the valley and gruff voices shouted, 'Anyboddle seed him? Anyboddle seed the unicorn?'

Sylvestro's fur stood on end. 'Trolls. That means trouble—'

'We've got to save it!' Bibi began scrambling down the hill as fast as she could. 'AAAAAAAGH!'

Bibi slipped, and she rolled over and over with a yell. Rubbing her bruised elbows she staggered to her feet, the mist a dense blanket around her. Shutting her eyes she listened intently and, when the horns rang out again, she hurried towards them.

CLANG!!

A set of jagged metal teeth crunched together, missing her by a fraction.

'Troll trap,' Sylvestro told her. 'Probably meant for the unicorn.'

Bibi looked at the trap in horror. 'But that would break its legs! It's horrible!'

'That's trolls for you.' Sylvestro shook his head. 'I suggest you proceed with care from now on. There's sure to be others.'

Sylvestro was right. Bibi had been scrambling up the unicorn's hill for only a few minutes when a heavy net swung down from the branches overhead. With a startled yell she hurled herself into the bushes to avoid getting tangled in its meshes.

'Ouch!' The bushes were prickly. 'They *really* want to catch the unicorn, don't they?' She picked a thorn out of her arm. 'Why do they want it so badly? Do they want to ride it?'

'I doubt it.' Sylvestro was looking around cautiously. 'I haven't heard a hunting horn for a while. Perhaps they're checking to see if it's been caught?'

'Then we ought to hide!' Bibi was both scared and excited. 'I want to see what they look like. I've never seen a troll. Can they climb trees?'

'They're too heavy to get very high,' Sylvestro said. 'But they're easily strong enough to seize a tree and uproot it.'

'Oh dear.' Bibi rubbed her nose. 'Look! There's a cave... it's small, but I think I could squeeze in.'

Sylvestro's whiskers were trembling. 'Better hurry. I can hear something coming...'

Bibi looked at him in surprise. The big black cat was usually so calm, but now his tone was urgent. As she ran towards the rocks he streaked ahead, and he was waiting for her as she wriggled through. Inside, the cave widened, and Bibi was able to stand and see out.

She was only just in time.

As the trolls came stomping between the trees, she gasped: they were twice as tall as she was and covered in strings of matted fur the colour of slime. Their eyes bulged, and their wide grinning mouths showed sharp yellow teeth.

'Net's come down!'

'Unicorn! Unicorn! Did we catch de unicorn?'

'Nah.' There was a grunt. 'Is nothing dere.'

Then came the sound of sniffing... and a growl. 'Been hooman here. I smells it!'

Bibi shivered. If they could rip up trees, could they force their way into her cave?

'Nah.' There was more sniffing. 'Dat isn't hooman. Dat is pussy cat, and king troll say pussy cat no good for pie. Little cracky bones and too much fluffiness. Unicorn is best for feast.'

The oldest troll licked his lips. 'More for king, more for us.' An unpleasant chuckle followed, and he went on, 'King troll wants unicorn horn to pick his teeth.'

Hidden in her cave, Bibi clenched her fists. The trolls wanted to *eat* the unicorn!

Another troll began to sing:

'Unicorn pie! Unicorn pie! Everyboddle love unicorn pie!

Catch it and cook it and serve it up hot

Munch it and crunch it straight out of the pot

Unicorn pie! Unicorn pie! Everyboddle –

AAAAGH!'

There was the sound of a hefty thump, and the song came to a sudden halt.

'That be Old Grandma Troll's song... don't sing!' This was followed by a loud wail, and Bibi, creeping forward, saw that the oldest troll had tears pouring down his mud-coloured cheeks. 'Grandma Troll is dead and gone!'

'Gone...' echoed his companions.

'Gone to tree top heaven!'

'Heaven...' came the echo.

'Never make de pie no more!'

'No more...'

'So no sing her song!' The singer was thumped a second time, and his tangled mane of hair grabbed to wipe away the oldest troll's tears.

The oldest troll took up his position as leader. 'Unicorn isn't caught yet. Set de net once more, then we check de other traps and de big pit on top of de hill.'

'What big pit?'

'Big pit by de palace where king troll is waiting.'

⋅*⋅

To Bibi, hardly daring to breathe, it felt like hours before the trolls finally had the net arranged. When at last it was done, they thundered away, muttering as they went.

Creeping out of her hiding place, Bibi stared at the plate-sized footprints. 'Wow! They were revolting.'

Sylvestro put his head on one side. 'So might you want to give up this particular quest?'

'Give up?' Bibi was horrified. 'Never!'

🐈

It was easy to follow the path the trolls had taken. Grass was trampled, branches snapped, and bushes flattened.

Higher and higher Bibi clambered, and as the wooded summit came into view she began to feel hopeful.

'The unicorn must have slipped away,' she told Sylvestro, but even as she spoke a triumphant blast from the hunting horn split the air.

'We got it! It's in de pit!' The cry echoed across the valley, and Bibi's stomach knotted. The trolls were huge and powerful; what could she do?

'Hurry, boys! Hurry! We got to see dis unicorn!' The voices were excited, and Bibi could hear the sound of heavy bodies crashing through the undergrowth ahead.

'I've got to save it,' she said. She shut her eyes tightly. *The trolls may be scary, but they're not at all clever...*

Sylvestro was looking at her with interest. 'You've had an idea,' he said. 'I know the signs.'

'I've got to trick them into letting the unicorn go,' Bibi said as she opened her eyes. 'The pit's at the top of the hill. I'm going to look around... and hunt for ideas.'

She set off at once. The trees grew close together, and she slipped from one to the next, moving as silently as she could.

It was a good decision. The troll guard was leaning against a sycamore, and she could easily have walked right into him. He was chewing on a twig and staring into space. Tucked into his belt was a heavy wooden club, studded with rusty nails.

Bibi froze. The guard stood, shifting from bristly foot to bristly foot and sighed.

'Where Hulk? I done my hours. Is his turn now.' He sighed again. 'Always late.' Bending down, he picked up a small log; as he lifted it to his mouth Bibi saw that

it was hollow and
had been hacked
into the rough shape
of a horn.

'HULK!'

It was all Bibi could do not to
jump and give herself away. The troll's voice boomed
through the forest so loudly that her ears rang.

'HULK!' he shouted again. This time he was
answered by a piercing whistle, and a second troll came
slouching towards him.

'You late,' the guard said crossly. 'Too late.'

Hulk slapped him on his hairy back. 'I been busy. De
unicorn is caught, Brutal. Tonight we feast!'

Brutal stared at him. 'Eh?'

'Unicorn is in de pit,' Hulk told him. 'Come see!'

'I can see?' Brutal dropped his wooden horn in
excitement. 'Where?'

'I told you! In de pit!' Hulk gave his companion a
shove. 'King troll say we cook de unicorn pie when de
moon comes up.'

Bibi shuddered. Time was running out. Hulk and
Brutal were marching away arm in arm, and she still

had no idea how to rescue the unicorn. Grabbing the
sycamore's lowest branch, she swung herself up and
began to climb; it was a tall tree, and she hoped that she
might get a glimpse of the troll king's palace.

·˙✳·˳·

Peering through the quivering leaves, she caught sight
of the hilltop. There was a ramshackle building with
crooked walls, and an untidy thatched roof sagging in
the middle. Bibi bit her lip. This had to be it.

A crowd of jeering trolls was leaning over a low
circular wall at the edge of the clearing; Bibi was certain
this must be the pit. A child troll picked up a pebble
and threw it, and when Bibi heard the unicorn whinny
in pain she knew she was right. The child troll laughed
uproariously, and others joined. Bibi clenched her fists.
'Why don't their mothers tell them to stop?'

Sylvestro, stretched out on a branch below, shook his
head. 'They're trolls.'

'They're cruel,' Bibi said fiercely. Then, as the
memory of the oldest troll's tears popped into her head,
'OH!'

She half slid, half jumped down to the ground. Seizing the wooden horn, she threw herself back up the tree but, once she was on the highest branch, she sat thinking.

'Grandma Troll... what did Old Grandma Troll sound like? I can't get it wrong! I'll only have one chance. She must have been very old...'

She put the horn to her lips and took a deep breath. She was so nervous it was easy to make her voice quaver as she called, 'Trolls! I b... b... be the g... g... ghost of Old Grandma Troll!'

The effect was dramatic. Every troll swung round, their eyes wide with shock. Bibi went on, 'L... l... listen to me! You be so c... c... clever to catch de unicorn!'

There was a faint murmur, and Bibi heard a trembling voice declare, 'It be Old Grandma for certain! Her did always go c... c... c... when she did talk!'

On the branch below, Sylvestro purred in relief.

'I do indeed b... b... be Old Grandma Troll!' Bibi tried to sound bold. 'I b... b... be in tree top heaven now... but I do see you.'

'Old Grandma Troll! Can you be seeing me?'

It was the little troll who had thrown the first pebble, and Bibi's scattered thoughts suddenly jigsawed together into a plan. 'I do see you! I seed you throw de pebble! Now... you dance me good luck dance before de feast.' She paused to try and swallow the lump in her throat. Would the unicorn understand what she was trying to do? Would her plan work?

Looking down, she found her audience nodding enthusiastically.

'Dance! Old Grandma Troll, we dance you de dance!'

·*·

There was no way back. As she was about to speak, the door of the palace opened. The troll who lumbered out was a walking mountain, with an enormous shaggy head.

'What going on?' he demanded, and his voice was so deep it could have come from the bottom of a well.

'Old Grandma Troll wants us dance de good luck dance!'

'Good luck dance before de feast!'

'We get big appetite for de unicorn pie!'

'Old Grandma Troll, she talk from tree top heaven!'

The troll king lifted his heavy head, and it seemed to Bibi that his sunken yellow eyes were looking into hers. His expression was unreadable. Would he stop her?

She could feel frogs doing somersaults in her stomach, and she made her decision.

'B... b... be ready! All trolls, each find BIG pebble and drop dem in de pit... but be sure you not hit de unicorn!'

She gave what she hoped was an evil troll-like cackle. 'Hee hee hee... de bruises spoil de pie! Then each troll do twirly whirly round and round and round again!'

'We do! We do de dance!'

And, as Bibi watched, troll after troll ran to pick up a stone and drop it into the pit. As she hoped, they were competitive: bigger and bigger stones were chosen, and the whirling and twirling that followed became wilder and wilder.

Bibi was holding the speaking horn so tightly that her knuckles were white. The pit was gradually filling up... but the unicorn was rearing, its eyes rolling as if it was terrified.

Did it realise what she was hoping to do? Was it playing a part?

·*·*·

The troll king, who had been silently watching, was the last to drop a stone. He had chosen the biggest on the hilltop, and came staggering towards the pit, dropping it with a mighty thump.

He stood back to be admired... and his face changed to thunder as he saw what he had done.

'RUN!' Bibi bellowed, but the unicorn was already bounding over the heaped-up stones. The king troll, arms stretched wide, let out a mighty roar, but it was hopeless. The unicorn flew like a snow-white bird across the grass, leaving the king shouting and cursing and stamping his feet. His fellow trolls thought he was encouraging them to be louder and faster in their dance, and ignored his shouts of 'Stop it! Stop it!'

Bibi all but jumped from her tree. The unicorn was standing waiting for her, tail twitching, and as she reached the branch above, it lowered its head in thanks.

'I'd suggest a speedy exit.' Sylvestro appeared. 'Can you ride?'

'Me? Ride the unicorn?'

The big black cat waved a paw. 'It's here for you.'

Bibi slid from the branch onto the unicorn's back, and away they went... the trees and bushes a green blur on either side as they sped down the hill and into the chill below.

At last the unicorn stopped, and shook the silver drops from its mane. Bibi slid off its back, and the unicorn dropped its head to nuzzle her shoulder. As it

did so, a tiny key fell into her hand... a key in the shape of a hunting horn.

'Thank you,' Bibi said and, greatly daring, she stroked its soft velvet nose. 'Go safely...' And the unicorn gave a loud triumphant whinny before galloping away.

As the sound of its hooves faded, Bibi saw that she and Sylvestro were standing beside a crumbling stone arch covered in prickly brambles. Curious, she walked through the arch to see what was on the other side… and gasped. There was no mist. A winding path led through bright green fields, and overhead the sky was clear.

'Let's go,' she said, and Sylvestro purred his approval.

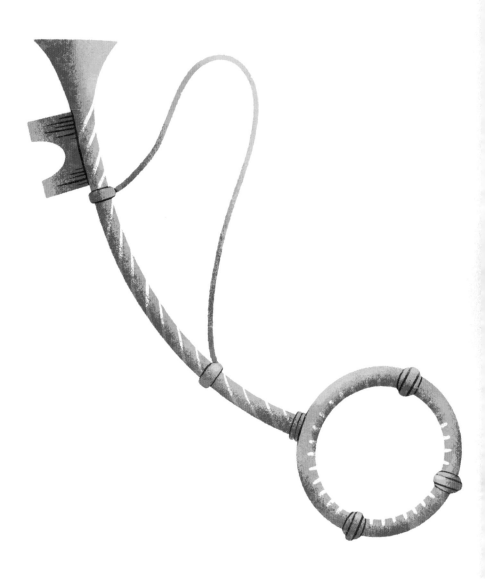

THE BLUE KING

fter Bibi had stepped through the arch, a movement caught her eye. Someone was hopping and jumping along the road towards her.

'Who's that?' she wondered out loud.

Sylvestro shrugged. 'A boy. A very ordinary kind of boy.'

As he came closer, Bibi saw that the boy's trousers were ragged and torn, but his coat was anything but ordinary – it was the brightest, most beautiful shade of blue. As he came closer, he waved.

'Hello! Have you ever seen a finer coat than mine?' And he twirled in front of her.

The boy looked so happy that Bibi couldn't help smiling. 'It's a lovely coat. Are you going somewhere special?'

The boy nodded. 'I'm off to the palace to visit the king. When he sees my fine blue coat, he's sure to give me a field of my own.'

'A field? Why do you want a field?' Bibi asked.

'For my family, of course! To grow potatoes and carrots, onions and cabbages... and maybe even to keep a goat!' His smile faded. 'We're very poor, you see.'

Bibi was puzzled. 'But why will the king give you a field when he sees your coat?'

The boy's smile came back wider than before.

'Today's his birthday, and he's celebrating by giving a field to the best dressed people in the land.'

'He doesn't sound like a very good king,' Bibi said doubtfully. 'Shouldn't he be looking after people, rather than worrying about what they look like?'

The boy gave a jump of excitement. 'That's why the court magician turned him blue!'

Bibi's eyes widened, and Sylvestro came closer. 'Blue like your coat?'

'Just like that.' The boy grinned. 'He offered the court magician a gold piece to make him handsome, but the magician told him good deeds were more important than good looks. The king was FURIOUS! He banished her from the kingdom, so then *she* got angry, and turned him blue... and he's been blue ever since.'

Maybe that's my quest, Bibi thought, *to sort this out.* To the boy she said, 'I think I'd better come with you. I'm Bibi, and this is Sylvestro... What's your name?'

'Gus Goodbody.' Gus tucked her arm through his and nodded at Sylvestro.

'Off we go!'

·˙✳·ᵧ·

As they hopped and skipped along the road, Gus told

Bibi about his family. He lived with his three little sisters and his mother, and he was very proud of them.

'My mam... she's a genius with a needle!' He let go of Bibi's arm so he could spin in front of her. 'See this coat? She made it from an old curtain!'

'It's a very fine coat indeed,' Bibi agreed.

Gus took her arm again. 'I'd have liked gold buttons, but they don't grow on trees. Maybe when I've got my field I can grow enough potatoes to sell at market, and then I'll have money to spend!' He glowed at the thought. 'I'll buy ribbons for my sisters, and a warm woolly shawl for my mam... and if there's any left over, I'll buy four gold buttons for me. And if you'd ever care to pop by, there'll always be a cup of tea waiting.'

'Thank you,' Bibi said. 'I'd like that. Although I'm not sure if I'll be coming this way again. I'm on a quest... but I don't quite know what it is yet.'

'I'll help you.' Gus gave her arm a squeeze. 'Look! We're nearly there!'

·˙✳˙·

He was right. The road had widened, and there were many more people about. As they turned a corner, Bibi saw tall golden gates, and a golden palace

glittering in the sunshine. Men and women were queuing in a long line in front of the closed palace gates, all dressed so brightly that Bibi blinked. There were pink and yellow striped dresses, green and orange spotted coats, purple and scarlet checked cloaks...

Gus's smile faded a little. 'I didn't know there'd be *quite* so many of us. Still' – his smile came back – 'nobody's wearing a coat like mine!'

'That's true,' Bibi said. She had noticed something strange, and she wasn't sure if she should point it out. People were dressed in all the colours of the rainbow – except for blue. Nobody was wearing blue. Not even a blue button...

'Gus,' she said slowly, 'have you seen—'

Bibi never finished her sentence. A huge hand seized Gus by the shoulder, and a gruff voice said, 'Treason! I see treason! Come to mock the king, have you? It's the lock-up for you, my lad – and you'll be lucky if you ever get out again!' And before Gus could say a word he was slung over the guard's burly shoulder and marched away, Bibi and Sylvestro scurrying behind him.

'Wait!' Bibi called. 'Wait! What's he done?'

'Done?' The guard stopped and stared down at her. 'Committed treason, that's what! Wearing blue? That's against the law! Where do you come from that you don't know that?' And he stomped off.

An old woman was standing watching, and Bibi turned to her. 'What's he talking about? How can wearing blue be against the law?'

'Sssh!' The old woman put her finger to her lips. 'It's His Majesty! Ever since he was magicked That Colour it's been banned.' She shook her head. 'That young lad had best hope it's a grey day when he comes before the king. He's always more cheerful then. Oh, dearie dearie me...'

Bibi didn't wait to hear another word. Hurrying after the guard, she was just in time to see him unlocking a heavy door at the back of the palace and bundling Gus inside.

'You'll see His Majesty later!' the guard told him, before locking the door and marching away, jangling his keys as he went.

As soon as the guard had gone, Bibi crept to the small, barred window. 'Gus! Are you all right?'

Gus's face appeared, and he wasn't smiling any more. 'Nobody told me the king wouldn't like my fine blue coat,' he said sadly. 'Now I'll never get my field... and what'll my mam do without me?'

'We've got to think of a plan,' Bibi told him, but Gus sighed.

'I'm no good at plans. Especially when I'm locked up.'

'Then I'll think of one,' Bibi told him.

·˙✳·˙·

Bibi was already working on ideas as she and Sylvestro walked away. 'Gus needs his field... so I need to find a way to make that happen,' she told the big black cat. She stopped to look in a shop window full of wonderfully bright hats and coats. A sign read, BY APPOINTMENT TO HIS MAJESTY, KING MORLANDO THE THIRD.

'So those are the colours the king likes,' Sylvestro remarked. 'Red and green and yellow and orange...'

Bibi walked on, still thinking.

The clip clop of hooves and the rumbling of a cart made the two travellers move to the side of the road.

'Bring out your blue!' The shout made Bibi jump, and she saw that the cart was piled high with cushions, rugs, lamp shades, tablecloths... and they were all blue.

'Where are you going?' she asked, as the driver pulled the horse to a halt.

'The rubbish dump,' he said. 'You got any blue?'

'No,' Bibi said firmly. 'Where's the dump?'

The driver pointed with his thumb. 'Edge of the kingdom.'

'I don't suppose' – Bibi's mind was whirling – 'that I could have that tablecloth?'

The driver's eyebrows shot up. 'But it's blue! If you're caught with that you'll be up in front of His Majesty, sure as that there horse has hooves!' He shook his head. 'More than my job's worth to give it you. On the other hand—' he gave Bibi a broad wink '—we don't close the dump until late tonight.' He cracked his whip, and the cart rumbled away.

'Let's follow him,' Bibi told Sylvestro.

'Do I understand you've had an idea?' the cat asked.

'I hope so.' Bibi crossed her fingers. 'If it doesn't work, I might be in prison with Gus for a very long time...'

The rubbish dump was not far away. Bibi waited until the driver had emptied his load; once he was out of sight she went to look. She felt sad to see so many things that must have been loved by their owners; how could anyone throw away a baby's tiny blue bonnet and a small blue bear?

'It's time that king changed his mind,' she told Sylvestro, and she climbed in to choose what she needed. At the last moment a child's paintbox caught her eye, and she picked it up to add to her collection.

'An interesting choice,' Sylvestro said, and Bibi sighed.

'I've *got* to help Gus. But how can I get back to the prison without being arrested?'

A large blue bag provided the answer; turned inside out it was grey, with no hint of blue. After stuffing it with her findings, Bibi and Sylvestro set off.

Gus was delighted to see Bibi again. He was even more delighted when Bibi told him she had a plan, but when she explained that it involved her getting arrested he looked worried.

'You should go home,' he said.

'I can't. I haven't completed my quest.' She glanced down at Sylvestro. 'Perhaps you should wait here.'

Sylvestro twirled a whisker. 'Miss Myrtle wouldn't like that at all.'

'Well... if you're sure.' Bibi turned to Gus. 'Are you ready?'

Gus nodded, and she pulled the blue tablecloth out of her bag. Swirling it round her shoulders she danced up and down outside the prison door, singing, 'Blue, Blue! Lovely blue! What would we do without beautiful—'

'Oi! That's enough of that!' It was a different guard,

but he was just as enormous as the first. Picking up Bibi and her bag as if she weighed nothing at all, he opened the prison door and half pushed, half threw her inside. Sylvestro, silent as a shadow, slipped in after her.

'His Majesty ain't happy, and that's a fact,' the guard said. 'He's heard as we've caught a rebel, and it's ruined his birthday. You'll both be seeing him at quarter past four after he's ate his tea, and you'd better get ready for trouble.' Having delivered this grim warning, he slammed the door.

Gus went pale, but Bibi stood firm. 'We're going to be all right. Trust me.' She opened her bag and took out the paint box. 'It's a good thing you've got blonde hair. Mine's too dark. But it's going to help you get your field!'

Bibi did her best to look as if she knew what she was doing as she and Gus waited for the guards to take them to meet the king, but her knees were shaking badly. As the door swung open she took a deep breath, swirled the blue tablecloth over her shoulders, and stood up as straight as she could.

'WHAAAAAT?' The guards stood frozen in the doorway, their eyes popping, as they gaped at the two figures in front of them. Bibi was draped in the blue tablecloth, with a blue tasselled lampshade on her head, but Gus was blue from head to foot. His face was blue, his hair was blue, his coat was blue – and one sock was light blue and the other navy. Bibi had been unable to find a matching pair.

'Stone the crows!' The largest guard finally got his breath back. 'You'll be lucky if you keeps your heads on your shoulders, looking like that!'

Bibi's stomach lurched unpleasantly, but she forced herself to smile. 'We're ready!' she said.

The walk through the marble corridors seemed endless. At every step Bibi felt more and more uncertain that her idea would work. Gus was holding her hand so tightly that her fingers hurt, and her mouth was so dry she wondered if she'd be able to speak at all.

·˙✳·ᵥ·

The golden doors to the throne room swung open with a crash.

The king was sitting on a pile of cushions... and his face was the same bright blue as Gus's coat.

'Your Majesty' – the guards had an iron grip on Gus and Bibi's shoulders – 'the rebels.'

The king stared.

Bibi and Gus stared back.

The king's eyes bulged, and his face turned an unpleasant shade of dark plum. He jumped to his feet, but he was so angry he was unable to speak – and Bibi stepped forward. She bowed so low that the lampshade was in danger of falling off; she rammed it back on and took a deep breath.

'Your Majesty!' she said, and her voice hardly shook at all. 'Your Majesty! We are your most sincere and humble admirers. We believe blue is the new and wonderful colour of the kingdom... to us, blue is the sky, blue is happiness, blue is YOU, our most noble king – and blue is – BLUETIFUL!' And she bowed, while her mind fizzed and buzzed at her mistake. *How could I have got that wrong?* she asked herself... but she couldn't say her speech again.

There was a long pause. Bibi and Gus held their breath. Hidden behind the throne, Sylvestro froze. The guards tightened their grip, waiting for the explosion... but none came.

·˙✳·˴·

The silence went on... and on... until the king sat back on his cushions.

'Call for the prime minister!' he ordered. 'Call my councillors! I have an important announcement to make!'

The guards looked at each other, then at the king. 'Did we ought to lock the prisoners up again?'

'Prisoners?' The king jumped up and ran to Bibi.
He hugged her, he hugged Gus... and then he shouted,
'These aren't prisoners! They're... they're BRILLIANT!
They have seen what nobody else has seen... that BLUE
IS BLUETIFUL!' And he held out his coat tails and
danced round and round in a circle. 'From now on the
kingdom will celebrate blue – Tuesday will become
Bluesday... and everyone – yes! EVERYONE! – will wear
blue in honour of ME!'

He stopped. 'I'll be the only blue king in the whole wide world... that makes me a very special king. And a very special king should be kind... and generous... and an example to his people. Tell me, young lady – tell me! How can I reward you? With gold? A dozen snow-white horses? A castle?'

'If you please, Your Majesty,' Bibi said, 'I'd like a field for my friend, Gus Goodbody.'

'DONE!' roared the king, and as the prime minister and the councillors came hurrying into the throne room, he ordered a paper to be signed giving Gus the finest field in the kingdom.

'Anything else?' the king asked. 'A field is a mere nothing!'

Bibi thought for a moment. 'Four gold buttons?'

'Easy peasy,' said the king, and he pulled four gold buttons off his velvet coat and handed them to her.

As the king settled down with his councillors, Bibi saw Sylvestro heading for the door. 'I think we should go,' she whispered to Gus, and he nodded. Clutching the paper, they tiptoed away.

Outside the palace Gus did a dance of joy. 'Thank you, thank you, THANK YOU!' he said, and he hugged Bibi tightly.

'And I too must thank you.'

Bibi and Gus spun round to see a tall woman in flowing robes smiling down at them. 'You've persuaded that foolish king to see a little sense at last.'

Bibi blinked. 'Excuse me... who are you?'

The woman laughed. 'I'm the court magician!

I turned the king blue... and he thoroughly deserved it!'
She looked down her nose. 'Wanting to be handsome...
really! But now – perhaps – he'll think about his people,
rather than himself.' And she handed Bibi a silver key,
covered with little blue stars.

'What's that for?' Gus asked, but Bibi knew.

Taking the key with a sigh, she said, 'I'm sorry, Gus.
I've got to go. I hope I see you again...'

A small round opening had appeared in the palace
wall... an opening that hadn't been there before.
Sylvestro looked at it suspiciously. 'That has the
appearance of a tunnel.'

'It does,' Bibi agreed. 'Let's see where it goes to...'

WiTCH PRUNELLA SPONGE

t was dark. So dark, Bibi felt she was wrapped from head to toe in the thickest of blankets. Was she in a tunnel, or deep underground?

'Can you see anything?' she asked Sylvestro.

'Of course I can. I'm a cat. We're at the top of a tower. The door's right in front of you.'

A smell of burning tickled Bibi's nose and made her sneeze. At once the door opened, and she was almost blinded by the sudden burst of light.

'I never meant to burn it, mistress – I didn't, I didn't, I didn't. OH! Who are you?'

Bibi rubbed her eyes. An agitated elf was hopping up and down in the doorway, holding a toasting fork.

On the end of the fork was something so burned she couldn't begin to guess what it was.

'I'm Bibi. Who are you?'

The elf trembled. 'She calls me Muddle 'cos I muddle everything. I'm sure she'll turn me into a toad, but I didn't mean it! I was watching her marshmallows when I saw a spider spinning a web and I wondered how it knew to go round and round and next thing they were BURNED!' Muddle dropped the fork on the floor and burst into tears.

Bibi, trying hard to understand the elf's flood of words, bent down to comfort him.

'Don't cry! Why don't you toast some more?'

'But there's a horrible smell,' Muddle wailed. 'And she'll be back soon – she's only gone to find toadstools and frogs. I didn't mean to burn it and she'll be so angry!'

'Hang on!' Bibi held up a hand. 'Who are you talking about?'

Muddle's mouth opened. 'The witch! Witch Prunella Sponge... Surely you've heard of her?'

178

Sylvestro gave a low growl, and Bibi shook her head. 'No... never. Why does she need toadstools and frogs?'

'To make spells. Normally she just watches stories in her crystal ball and eats toasted marshmallows... She loves it when the stories are about angry, unhappy people who end up even more miserable. But now *she's* the one who's angry! She's FURIOUS! Some girl's been spoiling the endings, and she's making an extra horrible spell to stop her!'

A chill crept down Bibi's spine. 'How do you mean, spoiling the endings?'

Muddle didn't answer. 'She'll be back any minute. If she finds I've wasted her sweeties she'll frizzle me up – oh dear, oh dearie, dearie me...'

'I'll show you what to do. My mum always burns the toast. In our last flat, we flapped things to stop the fire alarm going off. Have you got a tea towel?' And she followed the elf into the witch's room, Sylvestro close behind.

Inside, she stopped, stared… and forgot about the
tea towel. Thick black curtains kept out the sun, but
hundreds of tall pink candles flamed and shone, making
the room dazzlingly bright. The walls were shelved,
and each shelf was piled high with boxes and boxes
of sickly pink sweets. In the middle of the room was a
huge armchair heaped with cushions; beside it was an
enormous crystal ball gleaming in the candlelight. A
cauldron hung in the fireplace, the pink gloopy contents
bubbling sulkily, but Bibi's eyes were fixed on the ball.
Were those faint figures moving inside…?

·*·

Muddle pulled her arm. 'There's the marshmallows. I'm
sure she counts them. She'll know I've wasted some—'

'Indeed she will!' A deep plummy voice came from
the doorway. Bibi spun round to see a woman dressed
in black … and her jaw dropped. This witch wasn't like
the witches she had read about in fairy tales. She was so
pink she was almost purple, with a soft squashy look,
as if she was made from the marshmallows she was
so fond of eating. Her chins, dusted with icing sugar,
wobbled up and down and the whiskery wart on the
end of her nose quivered.

The witch was looking at her visitor with such an evil smile that Bibi felt her bones freeze. Behind her, crouched under a table, the fur rose on Sylvestro's back.

'I do believe it's little Miss Interference! Well, well, well... so *you're* the one who's ruined my stories!'

She grabbed Bibi's wrist. 'Let me show you what you've done, my little mushroom...' and she dragged her to the crystal ball. 'Watch!'

As Bibi peered into the glass, she gasped. There was Giant Glum sipping tea with the fairies and smiling happily in a valley full of flowers; as the image faded the witch ground her teeth.

'Disgusting! Revolting! Sickening!' Prunella Sponge sneered. 'I enjoyed watching that giant grow more cowardly by the day. I was sure he'd turn to stone for ever and ever... but what happens? You come skipping into the story... and what do you do?' She gave Bibi's arm a savage twist. 'You interfere! Think you've been doing good, don't you? Trailing through fairy tales and giving them happy endings!' She gave a huge sigh.

'How I enjoyed seeing that prince shut up in the tower! That stupid blue king! The pathetic sea elves! Those silly little gnomes digging and digging... and as for the trolls – oh, how I longed to see them catch that unicorn! That was the best story yet! Catch him and cook him and crunch up his bones. But—' She scowled darkly as she remembered how the story had ended. 'There wasn't a pie, was there? You were so clever, so cute, so cunning... so what am I going to do now? What can I watch?'

A sly look came over her face, and she pulled Bibi close. 'I was going to make a spell... a lovely little spell. Misery, failure, spiders and dust!' She pointed to the crystal ball, and to Bibi's horror she saw her own house... her house in the woods.

'You can't do that!' She clenched her fists. 'That's my house! It's not in a fairy story! Leave it alone!'

Prunella Sponge cackled. 'We're all stories, little mushroom! You spoiled mine... so I'll spoil yours! Since you're here, I've got a better idea. A much better idea!' She swooped to the door, locked it, and tucked the key down her dress. 'YOU can tell me fairy stories while I' – she flung herself into the armchair, her eyes gleaming – 'while I watch and listen!

And if you don't please me, little mushroom, then it's misery for you, and all who belong to you.' She turned to Muddle, who was cowering in a corner. 'What are you waiting for? I want mallows! Lots of marshmallows! I'm hungry... very hungry!'

Bibi swallowed. She was shaking. Nothing in her quests had been as scary as this.

'Ummm.' Could she remember 'Cinderella'? Bibi had loved the story when she was little, but as she grew older, she'd found it silly. She had made the same wish every night for a whole year... but had it come true? No. Bibi and her mother had to keep moving house, and no fairy godmother had ever appeared to offer them somewhere comfortable to live. That was when she'd decided that fairy tales were useless.

'Hurry up!' Prunella Sponge tapped her chair. 'I'm waiting!'

'Once upon a time,' Bibi began, 'there was a merchant who had a wife, and a kind and beautiful daughter—'

Prunella snorted. 'Would this be the story of "Cinderella"?'

When Bibi said yes, the witch told her to change the ending. 'Make sure the prince marries one of the ugly sisters, and that goody goody two shoes – well, one shoe—' Prunella roared with laughter at her own joke '—goes back to her empty attic with a broken heart.'

Bibi did her best. When Prunella demanded another story, she managed a garbled version of 'The Billy Goats Gruff', where the troll ate all three goats. As she came to the end, she was running out of ideas... and Prunella was getting restless. Twice she interrupted, and every time Bibi stumbled over a word she sighed heavily and rolled her eyes.

'Tell me another. A better one!'

Bibi was trying not to panic. *I've won six keys. I have to win this one too... but how? What can I do?* Beneath the table, hidden from the witch's view, Sylvestro gave Bibi a small, encouraging nod. It wasn't much, but it helped her think. *The pebble... I've got the magic pebble.* She slid

her hand in her pocket to check. Could she make herself small enough to creep under the door? What if the witch saw her shrinking, and stepped on her? Prunella Sponge would probably enjoy that.

'What are you playing with? Give it to me!'

'It's nothing,' Bibi's voice shook.

'Let me see!' Prunella ordered.

There was nothing Bibi could do.

'Here,' she said, and held out the pebble. 'Like I said... it's nothing. It came from the beach. I just... like playing with it...'

She had said too much. The witch's eyes sharpened, and she sat forward on her chair.

'Give it to me!' She snatched it from Bibi's hand.

Prunella said she had been watching Bibi's quests... what if she recognised the magic pebble? Bibi held her breath as she watched the witch turn it over and over.

A tiny squeak made her look up. Muddle had dropped his toasting fork – and his eyes were shining. He recognised the pebble... so why was he looking pleased that it was in the witch's hands?

Think, Bibi, think! she told herself. Muddle was an elf... and the pebble had been given to her by sea elves. Was there something she didn't know?

OH!

She'd had an idea... a wild and bold idea.

I'm not afraid, she thought. *I can do this! If I win the seventh key I can open the magic box, and* – her heart gave a leap – *maybe there WILL be a wish?*

Turning to Prunella, she smiled. 'Goodness! So, you *were* watching my adventures? You saw them in your crystal ball?'

Prunella gave a triumphant cackle. 'I saw everything, little mushroom!'

Bibi put her hands on her hips. 'Everything that happened?'

Prunella frowned. 'Of course!'

'Then you'll know that's the pebble the sea elves gave me... but I bet you can't remember the magic words! It took *me* ages to learn them.'

'You're only a human girl,' Prunella sneered. 'I'm a witch, and witches' memories are long. I remember the words exactly. *Pibble pebble, pobble pebble... AHA!*'

She heaved to her feet, eyes blazing. 'I see what you're up to! You're hoping I'll say the spell and shrink to nothing! You can't fool me... I'll teach you to try and get the better of a witch! *Pobble pebble, pibble pebble – make me TALL!*'

WHOOOOOOOOOSH!

Prunella grew... and grew and grew and grew. Through the ceiling she crashed, up, up and up. She gave one long piercing wail, but the cry was so high above Bibi's head it sounded like a seagull's call... and then –

BOOOOOOOOOM!

The witch exploded into thousands and thousands of bright pink marshmallows! As they rained down, Muddle gathered them up and shoved them into the cauldron, where they bubbled and popped to nothing.

'A most suitable ending.' Sylvestro came out from under the table, purring loudly. 'You did well.'

Bibi's legs gave way, and she sank to the floor. 'I never ever thought that would happen.'

Muddle giggled. 'That was clever! How did you know she'd make herself grow?'

'I didn't,' Bibi admitted. 'I was hoping she'd shrink, and we could catch her like a mouse. I should have realised she'd guess what I was up to.'

The elf bent down and picked the magic pebble off the floor. 'This is yours.'

Bibi shuddered. 'You keep it. It's dangerous!'

'It won't work again. It's cracked.' And, even as Muddle spoke, the pebble broke in half.

'That's a relief,' Bibi said. 'It's time to go. What are you going to do now?'

Muddle gave a skip. 'Go home!' He ran to the door, but it was locked... with a heavy iron bolt.

'Prunella had the key! We'll have to find another way.'

Bibi hurried to a window. 'Uh-oh. I didn't know we were so high...'

'We're miles up!' Muddle wailed, and he was right. The ground was so far beneath them it was shrouded in mist, and Bibi could hear the sound of the sea crashing against the rocks. The elf clutched her arm. 'What shall we do? We'll be here for ever!'

Bibi took a deep breath. 'I might have a friend who can save us.' Turning to Sylvestro, she unhooked a key from his collar. 'Mother Dragon promised to help me if ever I needed her.'

'A dragon?' Muddle stared. 'But dragons are scary!'

'Not this one.' Bibi held the key tightly in her hand and shut her eyes. 'Mother Dragon! Mother Dragon! I need you... PLEASE!'

·˙✳·˙·

For a moment nothing happened... and then the key began to glow. Brighter and brighter it shone, and Bibi smiled. 'She's coming! The magic's worked!'

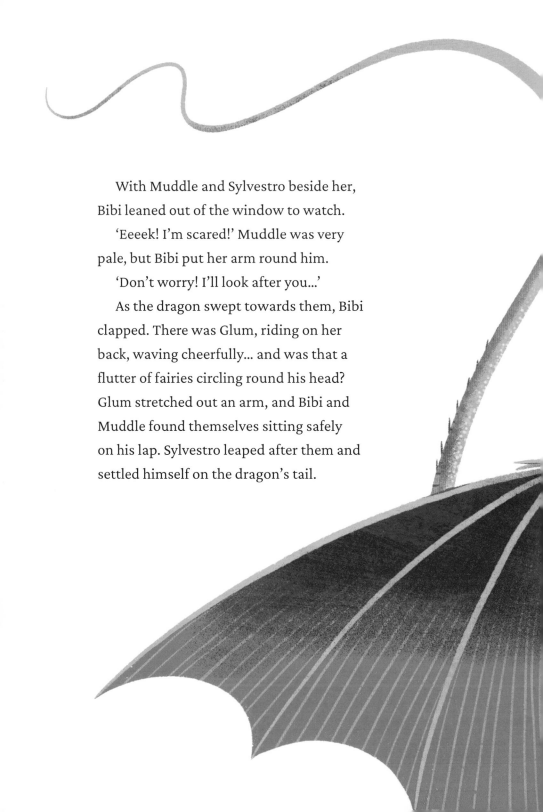

With Muddle and Sylvestro beside her,
Bibi leaned out of the window to watch.

'Eeeek! I'm scared!' Muddle was very
pale, but Bibi put her arm round him.

'Don't worry! I'll look after you...'

As the dragon swept towards them, Bibi
clapped. There was Glum, riding on her
back, waving cheerfully... and was that a
flutter of fairies circling round his head?
Glum stretched out an arm, and Bibi and
Muddle found themselves sitting safely
on his lap. Sylvestro leaped after them and
settled himself on the dragon's tail.

'Where to?' Mother Dragon asked, and Bibi leaned forward to whisper.

'Home it is.' And with a steady beat of her scarlet wings the dragon left the witch's tower behind.

Bibi, holding on to Glum's sleeve, looked down. There was the palace where the blue king lived – and Bibi smiled as she saw a boy in a sky-blue coat dancing happily along the road. Before she had time to wave, they were flying low over hills where the unicorn roamed... and then, she saw the gnomes' garden. As the dragon sailed over their heads, the gnomes threw flowers and cheered. 'We loves you, Bibi!' and Bibi blew a kiss to little Snubs.

On and on they flew... and there was the beach. The sea elves had made a new pattern of shells that said 'Thank you Bibi!'; they were too busy to look up, but Muddle gave an excited squeak. At once the dragon swooped down, and the little elf tumbled off her back and ran to join them.

The dragon soared higher... and now Bibi could see a royal procession. Prince Grandioso and his sisters were riding in an open carriage and, as the dragon's shadow fell across them, they stood and bowed and curtsied.

The dragon landed gently. They were in the field of
flowers that had once been a grey and windswept
valley. Glum, Bibi and Sylvestro slid off the
dragon's back and Bibi, greatly daring, stroked
her neck.

'Thank you,' Bibi said. 'Thank you so very
much!'

'The pleasure was mine, my dear.' And
the mother dragon spread her wings
and flew away.

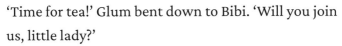

'Time for tea!' Glum bent down to Bibi. 'Will you join us, little lady?'

Bibi smiled. 'I'd love to... but I need to get home.' A sudden thought struck her, and she froze. 'Oh NO! I never got the seventh key!' She tried to swallow a sob. 'What... what did I do wrong?'

'Nothing.' Sylvestro came to stand beside her. 'Look at my collar...'

Wiping her eyes, Bibi looked and counted, 'One, two, three... four, five, six – SEVEN keys!' And she hugged the big black cat.

'Excuse me.' Sylvestro slipped out of Bibi's arms. 'If the seventh key is there, it's because you've earned it.'

'Thank you,' Bibi said. 'But how do I get home?'

At once the fairies clustered round her. 'This way,' they sang, 'this way!' Catching hold of Bibi's hands and clothes, they lifted her into the air. 'Home, home, home!'

Bibi felt herself float up into the air. All she could see was glittering wings, and all she could hear was the sound of singing. The glitter grew brighter and brighter, and she shut her eyes...

A MAGIC BOX

ibi's feet touched the ground with a bump. Opening her eyes, she gave a squeak of excitement. She was in the attic – and there, sitting very straight on her chair, was Miss Myrtle... or was it? This Miss Myrtle wasn't a faint shadow. She was as real as Bibi, and her blue eyes were sparkling.

'So! You're back! And how do you feel about fairy stories now?'

Bibi didn't hesitate. 'I love them! Well... maybe not the witches.' A thought came to her. 'I didn't meet any fairy godmothers, though. Why didn't I?'

Miss Myrtle laughed. 'Because I'm from your story... the story of a girl who had to earn seven keys in order

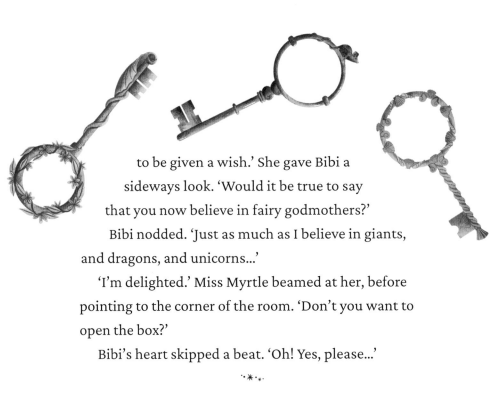

to be given a wish.' She gave Bibi a sideways look. 'Would it be true to say that you now believe in fairy godmothers?'

Bibi nodded. 'Just as much as I believe in giants, and dragons, and unicorns...'

'I'm delighted.' Miss Myrtle beamed at her, before pointing to the corner of the room. 'Don't you want to open the box?'

Bibi's heart skipped a beat. 'Oh! Yes, please...'

* * *

The magic box was glowing as Bibi kneeled down beside it. Carefully unhooking the keys from Sylvestro's collar, she began to open the locks one by one.

As each chain fell away, Miss Myrtle counted, 'Five... four... three... two... STOP!'

Surprised, Bibi looked up, the seventh key in her hand. 'What's wrong?'

'Nothing's wrong, dear. It's time you made your wish. And remember! You have only one, so choose wisely.'

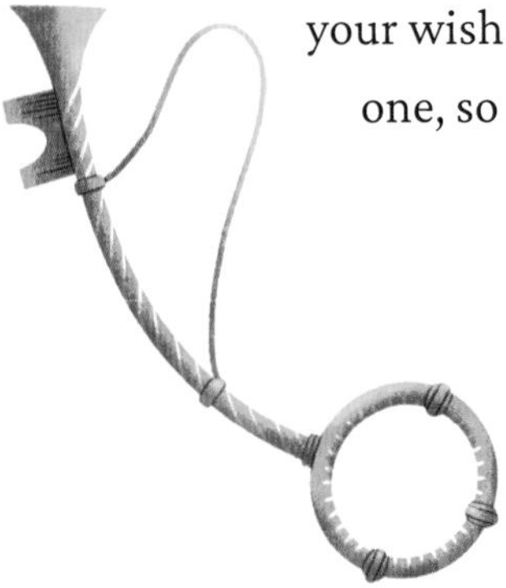

Bibi swallowed. She had met giants, dragons, elves and unicorns... and she had the keys to prove it. But a wish – the one thing she wanted more than anything else on earth – could that really come true?

'Well?' Miss Myrtle raised her eyebrows.

Bibi took a deep breath. 'I wish... I wish that me and Mum didn't have to keep moving. That we could live in the same place for a long, long time.'

'Good. And now... open the box.'

Bibi turned the key, the lock clicked – and slowly... slowly... she lifted the lid.

·˙✳·˙·

The box was empty.

·˙✳·˙·

Bibi stared, and stared again... how could the box be empty? But when she looked up to challenge Miss Myrtle, there was no one there. Miss Myrtle and Sylvestro were gone.

'Bibi! Bibi? Where are you?'

It was her mother's voice, and she sounded... different.

Slamming the lid of the box, Bibi jumped to her feet. 'I knew it was rubbish!' she shouted, and she dashed to the stairs, ignoring the soft chuckle that followed her. Down the stairs she scrambled and found her mother on the landing below, a letter in her hand.

'Bibi! You'll never ever guess!' Her mother's face was alight with happiness. 'This house! The owner has offered us a lifetime tenancy... oh, Bibi! We'll never need to move again!' She flung her arms round Bibi and hugged her tight. 'We must celebrate! Cake... I'm sure we brought some cake with us... oh, Bibi! Isn't it wonderful? It's as if a fairy godmother answered our wishes! Come on... let's see what we can find in the kitchen!'

Bibi's head was whirling. Was this how wishes worked? 'I'll be there in a minute,' she said. 'There's something I need to do first...'

As her mother hurried downstairs, Bibi climbed back up to the attic. She opened the door... and gasped...

·'·✳·'·

Pretty flowered curtains were hanging at the windows, a cosy little bed was tucked against the wall, soft rugs covered the floor... and an armchair heaped with cushions was waiting for her in the corner. On a table beside it was a pile of books... and they were all fairy stories.

Hardly daring to believe her eyes, Bibi patted the bed... It was real.

'THANK YOU,' she said, and once again there was a chuckle.

'Enjoy yourself.' It was Miss Myrtle's voice. 'And be happy!'

'Oh – I will!' Bibi promised. 'And thank you so, so much.'

'The pleasure is mine. And you might care to look inside the box. It wasn't quite as empty as you thought.'

The box was where Bibi had left it, and she heard a sound... the tiniest of meows. Crouching down, she lifted the lid and there, curled in a furry ball, was a coal black kitten with bright green eyes.

'Ooooooh,' Bibi murmured as she picked up the kitten and cuddled it. 'You're SO beautiful!'

The kitten purred loudly and snuggled into her neck.

'Let's show Mum,' Bibi said, and she carried the kitten down to the kitchen.

Her mother was singing as she laid out the cups and saucers.

'What's that you've got there? A kitten?'

'He was in the attic,' Bibi said. 'We can keep him, can't we?'

Her mother put her arm round Bibi. 'I'd say he's exactly what this house needs.'

As the teapot was put on the table, Bibi was certain she could hear footsteps. She ran to look... and was just in time to see Miss Myrtle walking briskly towards the front door, Sylvestro close behind.

'Wait!' Bibi called. 'Please wait!'

Miss Myrtle put a finger to her lips. 'Hush, child. My work here is done... and I have other things to do.' She shook her head. 'It's a busy life, being a fairy godmother. Perhaps you should consider it yourself? When you're a little older, of course.' She peered at Bibi over her spectacles. 'I think you'd do quite nicely. Give me a call when you're ready.' And then, as Bibi watched with wide eyes, she and the big black cat faded through the door... and were gone.